I0718755

Felix Publishing 2021
email: info.felixpublishing@gmail.com
Print copies available from publisher.

The Cry of the Currawongs

Print Edition
ISBN: 978-1-925662-44-3
Digital Edition
ISBN: 978-1-925662-45-0
Author: Dr Peter T. Scott

Registration:
Thorpe-Bowker +61 3 8517 8342
email: bowkerlink@thorpe.com.au

This is a work of fiction. The characters in this book did not exist and the politics of the time have been generalized. Some of the places described are real and are well-known to the author. No disrespect is meant to any person living or dead.

The Cry
Of the
Currawong
and Other Stories

Peter T. Scott

First released 2021

Contents

The Cry of the Currawong

It's funny how one little image or sound can invoke one's memory and bring back thoughts from the distant past. So it was that I was sitting in my study late one afternoon with a pile of term papers in front of me and little desire to start marking them. Term had finished last week and the students had all left for their holidays.

My thoughts were interrupted by a melodic warbling from outside my window. I stood up and walked over to the window and looked across the wide green expanse of the now deserted playing fields of the university to the blue hills beyond. There was a large pine tree not far from my window where two currawongs had made their nesting place.

Currawongs are dark-plumaged birds, being dark grey or black with large bills. They resemble crows and ravens, although they are slimmer in build with longer tails, shorter legs with white markings on their wings and tails. Apparently, they mate for life and both parents are very diligent in making a nest; in this case, in the pine tree near my building.

Perhaps their most striking feature is their cry, which can vary from a few short, sharp raucous calls to long, rambling warbles of a most melodic form.

I had not heard that sound for many years and now as the two birds were fussing around the base of their tree gathering sticks and leaves for their nest above, I returned to my chair, leaned back and closed my eyes to take in their song.

In the darkness of my mind, their warbling had transported me to a time in my distant past when I had first heard such a song. I was a very small boy, then and I had travelled on holidays from the city to the country. When was it? 1952 perhaps. I must have been all of seven years of age at the time and the many memories of those happy times came back to me.

The currawongs then had been nesting in a large Grey Gum which stood across the road from the house in which we were staying. It belonged to my mother's Aunt Hannah and had been built somewhere around the turn of the twentieth century by her young husband, Stan who now was well over eighty and spent most of his time bed-ridden in the front bedroom of the house.

I remembered how excited I was in hearing these birds warbling to each other for the first time. At home, back in Sydney, our birdlife seemed somewhat cheerless; sparrows mostly, who seemed to spend their days making pests of themselves and squabbling with each other in their haste to get on with whatever they were doing. Much like city people I imagined.

It had been a bad time for my mother and she needed this brief holiday. She had spent much of her meagre savings on the train fare. My father had died in the previous year, leaving my mother and I alone. We lived in a small, rented semi-detached house in the south of Sydney in a treeless street full of houses of the same monotonous construction. My father had worked in a paper mill a few miles[1] from our home and had been much older than my mother. I guess that the hard work and walking to the mill every day was just simply too much and his heart had simply given out.

My mother, as was the accepted thing in those days, had no job other than just 'keeping house' for her

____

[1] I use the old Imperial measurements in this book as would be appropriate at that time. 1 mile = approx. 1.6 kilometres. 1 yard = 0.9 of a metre and 1 foot = 30 cm, 1 inch = 2.54 cm.

small family of three. Now there was just a small Widows' Pension and some small amounts of money which my mother received by caring for the children of our neighbours who did go to work.

As a very young child, the impact of my father's death was not as great as that on my mother. Young children seem to be more resilient than adults. I guess that is part of some biological survival system which young people have so that they can at least make it to adulthood. I remember those days very well. Perhaps that is also part of that biological survival kit. I remember my very first day at school, for example. There was a long corridor of large windows on one side with wooden racks for school bags below. On the other side of the corridor were the windows and doors of the classrooms. My mother was holding my hand tightly, reluctant to let her only child go into another's care, as she talked to the Headmistress about my future. Passing an open door to one classroom, I shook my hand free from that of my mother and ran into that glorious room. It was full of small tables and chairs, coloured circles of carpet on the floor, posters of animals and other interesting things on the wall. There was also a large blackboard which ran the entire width of the room. There was some chalk still left on its tray and I picked it up and began drawing. The Headmistress gently ushered me out of the room and back to my teary mother who knew now that her son had found another world.

It was a few years before my father died and I was about four years old. My mother then was a very outgoing lady of middle age with a ready smile and happy laugh. She seemed to always have a ready answer for any of my young problems and nothing was impossible. She had many friends in our 'working class' neighbourhood and she had been the only girl in a large family of brothers who also had relied on her to solve their many problems.

Her joy of living had now suddenly vanished. With her husband now gone, the only thing that mattered was caring for her only son. Her spirit was now one of sadness and her loss almost too much for her to bear. She never smiled now and whilst she still had many friends, and her brothers and their families visited more often than before, nothing much seemed to give her any happiness.

It was near the end of the year as I recall, when she had a letter from her Aunt Hannah who lived in Yass, a small township on the Southern Tablelands about two hundred miles southwest of Sydney. Her aunt invited us to go and spend Christmas with her and her invalid husband, Uncle Stanley. Aunt Hannah had been Mum's favourite and the youngest of her mother's sisters. My mother had grown up in Yass, her father being the local blacksmith. She often told me that she and her many brothers had lived in a great stone house down near the river. Times had been hard for them too, as the trade of blacksmith was dying out in the country with the advent of the motor car. Her father and her brothers, who naturally were apprenticed into the family business as soon as they could get out of school, had little choice but to move to Sydney where they could find work.

I had never been on a holiday before; my father's work did not really allow for such extravagances but then I did not really understand that many people often left their homes and went somewhere else to play and have fun. Visiting my uncles, who lived in various parts of the outer suburbs of Sydney, were the only travels which I had made until that time.

My mother was entitled to a rail ticket once a year on her Widow's Pension and she had saved some money for my ticket and the few expenses which we would incur on our trip. Now we were on that great passenger train which sped through the dingy, graffiti-covered back fences of the city before bursting out into the open fresh air of the country. The Riverina Express ran between Sydney and Albury, a distance of about three hundred miles but our destination, Yass Junction, was only a small station on the main line about a little more than halfway. The State governments of New South Wales and Victoria had built their railways using different gauges and so passengers going on to Melbourne, the capital of Victoria would have to get off the express and carry their baggage across the border to join another train going to Melbourne; such were the rivalries between the states of Australia. Now the Riverina Express was a crack passenger train at that time, consisting of about eight air-conditioned maroon and yellow-striped carriages including a Dining Car. It was hauled by a great, green steam locomotive, which, to my young mind was the most exciting object that I had ever seen.

On the platform at Sydney's Central Railway Station, my mother had taken me down to the front of the train to see this great machine. To me, it was a great steam-breathing beast; sitting panting great bursts of steam, impatient to start its long journey south. Its body was green, long and sleek and at its front there were two air vents like long eye slits above a pointed nose containing a large headlamp. Its engineers were leaning out of the great cabin enjoying their fame as the controllers of this beast and I thought that being a locomotive engineer must be the best job in the world.

After many hours of adventures exploring the long, wood-panelled carriages, especially the Dining Car where Mum and I had lunch, the train finally pulled into Yass Junction for a very brief stop. Naturally, I was afraid, like all small children, that my mother's delay in getting our suitcase down from its upper luggage rack would mean that the train would start again before we could get off. But we had plenty of time, because the engine had to take on more water here as well.

There was nothing much at Yass Junction but the railway station, a house for the Station Master and a few sheds. Beyond the station buildings in all directions was a vast plain of wire fences and dry brown grass dotted with the occasional small group of olive-green trees. I had some apprehensions that this might be our final destination.

Mum had picked up our battered old brown cardboard suitcase, held tightly together by a long leather strap, before walking off towards the end of the platform.

"Come along, Thomas," she said understanding my distress at not finding myself in the thriving township of Yass. "We must get the tram into town."

We walked around to the other side of the railway station to find another set of double railway track. Standing there were two small carriages; one for passengers and another with its wide, sliding door open, was for baggage. Two men in railway uniform with rolled-up sleeves were now loading this baggage car with boxes and the suitcases of passengers who had just alighted from our express train. Of greater interest was a small, black tank engine which was now puffing its way in reverse up to the passenger car. Both carriages seemed to me to have come straight from some western movie. They had windows which slid up and down and small metal-grilled balconies at either end. They were the sort of carriages that Bushrangers or Wild West train robbers would easily jump onto from their horses and then yell "stand and deliver!" or "hands up!" to their unfortunate victims cowering onboard. It is sometimes the case that progress often takes a retrograde step when governments take a hand. I recalled much later when I boarded the National Capital Express in Sydney as a callow youth of nineteen to take up my first teaching appointment in our nation's capital, that its carriages were very similar to these and that they were being hauled by a rather grubby, evil-smelling oily diesel engine.

We walked across a railway track and handed our precious suitcase to the two men who were loading the baggage car. The climb into the other carriage was difficult, as the steps did not quite make the ground, but with some help from my mother, I made it up onto the small balcony platform and into the carriage. I was familiar with the word 'tram' as Mum would take me to school every day on the tram which ran past my school back home. This was altogether a different sort of tram; electrically-powered and having only one carriage which ran down the centre of the city streets. Later when we finally came into the township of Yass not too many miles away, I found that this little steam train and its two wild west carriages also ran down the middle of the street as the town tram.

We climbed down from our carriage when it came to a stop near some railway buildings and Mum said that we would get a taxi out to where Aunt Hannah lived. Our taxi also was unlike those which I had seen in Sydney, for this was simply a black private car with neither labels on the doors nor any illuminated 'taxi' sign on its roof. Country life was going to be much different from what I had expected.

To my surprise, we drove straight through the town! We drove down a very wide street and past a few grand stone buildings and many shops which opened out onto a wide, covered walkway on each side of the street. I couldn't help but be reminded of towns in the many Hopalong Cassidy[2] western movies which my mother had taken me to see at the cinema. Not far out near the end of the main street, we veered off onto another road which was not paved at all but made up of compacted dust. I had never been on a dirt road before and was fascinated by the clouds of dust which came up from the car's wheels.

---

[2] A popular fictional western cowboy hero of movies and later television (1948 – 52).

A short distance up this road we were now in open country when the car suddenly stopped near a low, green hedge. In the middle of this hedge was a small gap which was flanked by two tall poplar trees and between them was an old picket gate of worn timber which had once been painted green.

The taxi driver took our battered old suitcase out of the car's boot and placed it on the ground near my mother. There had been a set fee which Mum had paid so he drove off. Picking up our suitcase, Mum pushed the old gate open and we walked into the front yard. The house in front of us was a simple, single story affair with a low, covered wooden veranda running across its front. Across this wide veranda with its cracked and broken boards was a central wooden door with an ornate stained-glass window at its top and there were two broad windows set in the wall on either side of the door. The wall seemed to be of plaster and any previous paint work had now faded into a dull light brown colour. Later, my mother explained that the house had been built by Uncle Stan and his friends when he married Aunt Hannah over fifty years ago. She said it was of 'wattle-and-daub' construction and it had two chimneys along one side and a rusty corrugated iron roof on top. There was a glass-fronted sign hanging next to the door which read 'Auchenblae' and I later found out that this was a place in Scotland, where Uncle Stan's people had originally come from over one hundred years ago.

The door opened and a large, happy-faced lady with a broad smile came out; her arms held open wide ready to embrace my mother. Mum put our suitcase down and hurried to the woman's embrace; tears flowing down her face.

"Welcome home," said the lady giving Mum an extra hug. She stopped and looked down at me with a smile:

"Well, now! This must be little Thomas and you must call me Nanna," with that, she bent down and gave me a broad hug which almost squeezed all of the wind out of me. "Come inside, now and I'll make us a fresh pot of tea. There's fresh milk from Cousin Horace's farm for little Thomas. Your Uncle Stan will be mighty pleased to see you both".

We were ushered into what Nanna called the front parlour, which I was to find out later was the biggest room in the house. We followed her into the smaller front bedroom where an old man was sitting up in a huge four-poster bed reading a newspaper. He put it down and looked over his glasses, a broad smile came across his gaunt face:

"Welcome Elle!" he said to my mother. "I hope that you can stay awhile and give an old man some company," he said in a strong voice that seemed out of place coming from such a thin, white face.

"Enough of that!" laughed Nanna, "and here is your grandnephew Thomas," she said standing away from the bed so that Uncle Stan could look over its side to the small boy standing uncertainly at its edge.

"Well! What a fine boy, Elle!" he said, looking up at my mother. "It'll be good to hear some childish laughter here for a change. Your Uncle John and his son Clarence moved out long ago."

Nanna ruffled Uncle Stan's pillows a little and gave the old man a comforting wink. "I'll bring you in a nice cup of tea presently, so you can get back to your sports pages. But there'll be no horses running this Saturday at the showground, mind."

We followed Nanna out of the room, past another small bedroom where Mum quickly put down our suitcase, then down a step into the kitchen.

It certainly was nothing like our kitchen at home! Almost taking up one outside wall was a huge black stove set into a large brick fireplace. It had a wide enamelled green door which was now closed and to its left was a small grated opening in which a small fire was burning.

"This is a fuel stove," Mum said, "and it will be your job to fetch wood chips to keep it going." This was a revelation to me because our stove at home was a smaller, upright contraption which worked on gas and was lit only when we needed it. This fuel stove had to be kept going most of the day so that our meals could be cooked on it. There was also a large, black water urn sitting on one side of the broad, metal top of the stove in which water was continually heated and then replaced through a lid at its top. A small metal pipe came out of the back of the stove and went up into the brick chimney above it.

Nanna took a large black kettle from the top of the stove and went over to the small white enamelled sink near the back door and filled the kettle with water which came from a large, corrugated water tank just outside. Placing it back onto the stove, she threw a few small pieces of wood from a metal bucket nearby into the fire and then stood up and looked at me.

"Come, Thomas. We will get you some fresh milk from the safe." With that she went out of the open back door, down another step and onto another veranda which ran the entire width of the back of the house. I was perplexed at the use of the word safe. I knew from school that a safe was where one kept valuables and money, like at the big bank up the hill at home.

Nanna went over to a tall, box-like structure which had its thin wooden frame standing in small cans of water. The entire structure was covered in some sort of loosely-woven cloth; hessian was what Nanna called it.

"This is our Coolgardie Safe, Thomas. We use it to keep our food cold as we don't have any electricity in this house, so we don't have a fridge".

She went on to explain that there was a shallow. open water tank up on top of the safe with strips of Hessian hanging down the sides from it onto the safe's walls. When the wind blew through the wet Hessian, the water evaporated and cooled down the contents of the safe. To me, this was a wonderful invention and I was surprised how cold the milk was when I tasted it.

When we went back inside Nanna gave me a slice of thick homemade bread and a small, wire fork made out of twisted coat-hanger. She showed me how to impale the bread onto its prongs and then toast it in front of the fire behind the metal grill of the stove. I was very careful not to burn the bread, so I would take it away from the fire now and then and look at the progress that I had made with the toasting. Eventually, it was nice and brown on one side. I then had to carefully pull the slice from the prongs and then turn it over so that the other side could be toasted. This having been done, I proudly took my toasted slice over to the table where Nanna had prepared a plate for it and opened a small silver cover on the butter dish which she had also brought from the safe. It was rock-hard but I was able to peel off several slices of butter and spread it, rather unevenly, onto my toast. It tasted scrumptious;

perhaps the best buttered toast that I had ever tasted. Far better than what we made at home in our little silver electric toaster.

Nanna had poured Mum a cup of tea from the little silver teapot which was covered with a multi-striped, woollen tea cosy to keep the tea inside warm. My mother took it and sat quietly at the end of the table.

"It's good to have you back, luv!" Nanna said. "You had some great times when you were here as a youngster."

Mum nodded with a blank look on her face, a common expression in response to others. Nanna continued:

"Do you remember when you and our Johnny were playing darts one morning? Stan had put up a huge dart board on the back of the outhouse and you and Johnny were throwing those little darts at it."

The outhouse so mentioned, was the outside toilet; a simple metal drum placed below a low bench with a wooden toilet seat and cover placed above it. It was set well down the hill towards the creek which gurgled along at the bottom of Nanna's property. The outhouse or dunny as it was called, was reached by a narrow, well-worn track which ran down from the house through high grass and thorn thickets. There were the usual warnings which went with the introduction to such a place, which included checking for redback spiders under the seat and snakes lying on the track. Nanna continued her story:

"I'm sorry to say that you were not very good at the game and you hit the outhouse more than the board."

There was just another nod from my mother.

"Do you remember? Johnny must have had a 'call of nature' or simply got bored with the game, because he threw his darts casually into the board and went to 'do his business' in the dunny whilst you continued trying to hit the board. Stan and I were having tea, just like we are now, when we heard a loud scream from the yard. It was Johnny in the dunny. He had thought that he had been bitten by a redback but in in fact it was simply one of your darts. It had passed through a gap in the dunny's old timber wall and had speared him in his bare bottom.

What a sight we encountered when he rushed out!
There was our Johnny, trying to hold his pants up
with one hand and waving a dart in the other. The
look of mixed indignation and alarm on his face was
a sight to behold. Stan and I thought that it was the
funniest thing we had seen for a long while".

My mother smiled. It was the first time that I had
seen her do so since my father had died those many
months ago. Now I knew that my loveable, happy
mother had finally returned. She and Nanna went
on reminding each other of some of the more
humorous happenings of her childhood here in Yass
and soon both women were in fits of laughter.

That was when I heard for the first time the raucous
cry and melodic warbling from the big gum tree
which stood in front of the house – the happy cry of
the currawong.

Life at Auchenblae

Country life was certainly greatly different to what I was used to in the city. Apart from the clean openness of the surrounding country, Aunt Hannah and Uncle Stan still lived in much the same way as they had done in the early part of the century. In the town and out on most of the properties, people had electricity and some more modern forms of sewerage but not here. Water tanks were still the most common supply of fresh water and I soon found out that it was different to that which I drank back home. It took me a few days of 'stomach problems' to get over the new bugs in the tank water.

Washing at Auchenblae was also different. At night, a large, oval metal tub was brought in from the back veranda where it hung on a wooden peg before being placed on the floor in front of the fire of the fuel stove. Nanna would then fill it with very hot water from the large, black urn on the stove and then cool it down with water from the outside tank. This she brought in using a large wooden bucket and poured the water into the tub until the water temperature was just right. A large cake of soap was tossed in and a very fluffy towel was hung over the back of one of the kitchen chairs.

"Time for your bath, Thomas." Nanna would say and then she and my mother would retire to the front parlour and close the door to the kitchen. I would be left to then strip off and climb into the tub which was of a size that it could easily hold an adult. The women folk apparently bathed later using the same principle and any men about would retire to the front veranda for a smoke or in my case to the mysteries of the front parlour. There was something very comforting about washing in a tub sitting in front of a warm stove with its little open fire door.

Back home in Sydney we had a geyser, or bathroom heater that was fired with town gas. To me, having a bath in our big enamelled bathtub was usually a dangerous affair. Firstly, I would have to turn on the water tap, cold being the only option, and then the gas. I would then quickly strike a match and then quickly light the pilot light nozzle and turn it around to light the large gas ring inside under the water tank. If the match was slow to light or I was delayed in any way in lighting the gas, there would be a loud 'whoosh' and the gas ball which had accumulated inside the device would suddenly ignite all around the base of the heater. Scary stuff for a small boy. One then would have to adjust the water and gas flow so that the appropriate temperature was achieved in the trickle which ran into the bath. After having the bath, one then also had to remember to turn the gas off before turning off the water. Having a lovely warm bath in a round tub with water from the urn was much easier to use and the room was warm as well; not like those cold winter nights cowering below in a shallow puddle of warm water in our bathtub back home!

For general washing of hands and faces, there was a long table set against the wall on the back veranda near the water tank. There were small wash basins standing in a rack on this table, near the row of pegs where one could hang one's towel. A large soap dish sitting on the bench contained some hand soap for face and hands. In the morning, one would wander out through the kitchen with a towel, which was usually kept on a bedpost, before going out onto the cold flagstones of the back veranda. Water was poured out of the water tank into one of the small basins for a quick wash. When finished, the water would be then thrown out onto the small garden nearby. Winter time was unpleasant in so much as both the air, water and flagstones were often below freezing point. If someone had been careless and had not emptied the wash basin the night before, the layer of ice would have to be broken before its water could be thrown out. Usually, covered in a thick dressing gown, woollen jumper and beanie, socks and slippers, one would quickly open the back door and dash out to partially fill a wash basin and then retreat just as quickly back to the warmth of the kitchen. Here some hot water could be added from the stove urn and the basin taken to the bench near the kitchen sink for a more humane wash.

Washing our clothes and bed linen was also a different affair. At home we had an electric washing machine in our little laundry which did all of the work and had a wringer above it. This would be used to squeeze out any surplus water once the items were rinsed in cold water in a large concrete washing trough nearby. Here in the country, we had a big 'copper' which was a tall-sided, open metal tub outside. A fire would be stoked in the metal box below and the water inside would be heated. The washing and a generous handful of powdered soap flakes would be thrown in. One then would actively poke and stir the sudsy mass with a long wooden paddle for some time; a very difficult task. Stained items could also be given extra attention by using a washing board; a slatted board upon which the stained item would be scrubbed with a large cake of raw soap and a big hand-held scrubbing brush. The washed item would then be soaked in the usual double concrete trough sitting next to the copper and then put through the ringer which had been clamped to the end of the trough. As at home, the items would then be pegged up onto a clothes line, which ran between two tall poles, to dry in the wind and sun. This chore usually happened every Saturday morning and involved both Nanna and Mum. It was hard going.

My daily workload was not very difficult for a small boy. I was in charge of gathering wood chips in an old, galvanised iron bucket from the large wood pile by the side of the house to ensure that the fire in the fuel stove was kept going. I would also responsible for feeding the fire to keep it going during the day. This was a great delight for a seven-year-old who normally would not be allowed to play with matches except for the explosive ignition of the bathroom geyser at home.

The other task I had was more adventurous. This was to gather eggs from the many nests which Nanna's free-range chickens had made in the long grass out the back of the cottage. They did have a chicken house which they would go into at night of their own accord, but during the day, they roamed within their own territory not far from the other side of the house. Here, the old paddock, which had once had green grass and a few cows to keep it short, now had become overgrown with long, yellow grass interspersed with many small thistle bushes; the cows and someone to tend and milk them had long gone. I would have to carefully walk though this long grass, which came well past my knees, along some of the small tracks which the chickens had made to find their nests. On most days, I would be able to find up to a half dozen eggs in the many small nests hidden in this grass. Mum had warned me about snakes as they also had an interest in the chickens and their eggs. There were foxes and stray dogs about as well, but they did not seem to be much of a problem close to the house where the chickens were mainly kept. Nanna also kept a small hatchery on the back veranda made from a large wooden box which was partly covered with a high timber roof. The fertile eggs she obtained from a neighbour, who had the only other house in the vicinity across the road, who had the rooster which would wake us up on most mornings. Nanna would keep the eggs and later the hatchlings, warm with a rubber hot water bottle wrapped in an old towel.

There was always something to do at Auchenblae for a small boy; apart from my daily chores. Much of the old farm still existed although in a rather run-down condition. There were the old stables which once had a stall for their old horse and his hay and a garage for their two-wheeled sulky. The old horse had been put out to pasture after years of good service and had then died at a very advanced age. The sulky was still there with all of its accoutrements such as leather harnesses and covers. This part of the stable held a wealth of new exploration possibilities for a young city boy. There were items of leather and brass which were a complete mystery to me and rows of tins with nails, bolts and other bits of metallic items such as horse shoes. Bottles of liniment and patent medicines, drenches for horses and cattle and weed killers stood forlornly covered in cobwebs along the high wooden shelves.

There had not been much attempt at maintaining the farm since Uncle Stan had suffered from arthritis and became bedridden. Their son, John – Uncle Johnny to us kids – left home as soon as he could, for a less-arduous work load by working for the

Country Roads Department. He had moved into an old house in the town which he shared with his son Clarence, who also had just started work for the CRD. Clarence, whom everyone called Boof, a reference to a rather dull cartoon character Boofhead who appeared in a comic strip in the local newspaper was an outgoing, bulky youth with a limited degree of thought. Even Nanna admitted that her grandson, whom she loved very much, was not the sharpest nail in the box but he grew up to be a big, happy soul who always meant well and so was popular with everyone.

My day was usually very busy, exploring the old sheds and the creek down at the bottom of the hill out the back of the old homestead. It was all new to me as my experience had mostly been the streets around our house in Sydney and in my schoolyard.

At home, I had several good friends who lived nearby who attended the same school, so Mum would let me go with these older children by ourselves to school, after all, they were one whole year older than I. Children seemed to be more adventurous in those days and parents, whilst still caring for the safety of their children, gave them much more freedom to roam far afield.

Here at Auchenblae, after my daily adventures, often with some of the local children who had become my friends, I would return home to find Nanna and Mum busy in the kitchen which was the main living space of the house and the focus of all social activity. I would make sure that I did not wander too far as I had the important duty of keeping the fuel stove going during the day. This meant going out and collecting wood chips in the old metal bucket and then coming in a stoking up the fire. Of course, I had to remember to close the door on the firebox and check that there was sufficient water in the old black urn on top of the stove so that it would not boil dry.

As the sun went down, Nanna would light the hurricane lamp. I have never found out why it was called this name but it gave a very bright light. She would fill its tank with kerosene and then pump the small plunger on the tank to pressurise its contents and then light the delicate white mantle which sat precariously inside its glass cylinder at the top of the lamp. She would replace the green metal shade over the top and place it in the centre of the large kitchen table.

I usually sat in one of the kitchen chairs reading one of the magazines which my mother had bought for me or one of the many interesting old picture books which Uncle Stan had kept in his small library in the front parlour. These were fascinating as they had old plates or printed black and white photographs or etchings of various exotic parts of the worlds with small descriptions of people and the customs of these distant lands.

Mum and Nanna went about preparing the evening meal which was similar to what we had at home – usually some form of meat dish and three vegetables such as potatoes, carrots and cabbage or beans. Somehow, the meals all seemed to taste so much better when they were cooked on a fuel stove; I now thought that our little gas stove at home was really a poor substitute for cooking.

After dinner, Nanna or Mum would clear the table and use some water from the urn to wash up the dishes and I would help to dry them with an old checked tea-town which hung on a nail above the sink. Uncle Stan in the early days of this homestead had rigged up a metal pipe which took the used suds out of the building below the flagstones of the back veranda and out into the garden beyond.

When this chore had been done and the dishes and pots put away, the table would be cleared and Mum and Nanna would sit down and knit or sew whilst they chatted about the day's events or about family gossip. I would read or play with some of the boxed games which Nanna had kept for her grandchild and the other younger members of her extended family. Usually, the day's activities would be most tiring and so about eight o'clock the bath tub would be filled, I would be left alone in the kitchen to bathe and put on my pyjamas and then Mum would light the candle in the little, squat candlestick holder that reminded me of a cup and saucer stuck together, and take me to the big four-poster bed with its soft, down quilt and tuck me into bed. The candle would be placed well out of my reach on the ornate dressing table across the room. She would give me a goodnight kiss and return to the kitchen. Sleep usually came very quickly and was a happy end to the day.

Nor was the day usually free for Nanna and Mum as there seemed to be a constant stream of people coming to the house simply to visit Nanna and Uncle Stan as well as to meet her new house guest. Word went around very quickly in a country town. Nanna did not have a telephone, few people did even back home in our street, but everyone seemed to know what everyone else was doing. There were no family secrets in those days.

Most of the people coming in were related to Nanna in some form or other and so many were also relatives of my mother; people she had not seen in over thirty years. By association, they were also my distant relatives too, and so my Mum proudly introduced me to everyone and I soon lost track of who was related to whom, or the son or daughter of, or just friends of. They also came in all ages; my mother's few aunts who still lived in the town were very elderly ladies of a bygone era, smelling of scented perfumes, powder and soap. Kissing elderly aunts soon became an unpleasant experience to a small boy who generally agreed with the rest of his peers that kissing girls, especially elderly aunts, cousins and so on, was just nor done.

There was also a sizeable group of these relatives who were closer to my age and I was welcomed into their secret world of fun, games and exploration. I soon lost track of how they were related to me, if at all, but that did not matter for we all seemed to get on well with each other. People in those days were more apt to be kind and friendly and preferred to play together rather than to try to 'own themselves' and have distant 'friends' only contactable through the Internet.

I soon worked out that here in the country there were three main groups of family members; aunts, uncles and cousins. The wider mob of visitors was also broken up into several subgroups. All adults who belong to the family or were close friends to it but not necessarily related to it, were addressed as Uncle or Aunt. Any other adult who was known to the family but not considered in its sphere were addressed more formally as Mister, Misses, or Miss. So old Harry who often visited his good friend Stan but was not related to anyone in the extended family was still called Uncle Harry by all those who were younger than him, including my mother. The baker who came out from the town in his horse-drawn baker's cart was called Mr. Dibbs as he was on a friendly but formal relationship to those at the house and was addressed by this name by me as well. He was a friendly man and would come out this long way very early in the morning so that his bread was usually fresh and still warm because he kept a charcoal-fed metal box inside of his closed cart. As a favour to me, he would let me have some of the warm, flaky crumbs which fell down onto the scrubbed wooded floor of his cart.

I also found that there was also a hierarchy within the children who I was regularly meeting. Most were generally called cousins regardless of their family status. Some had achieved adulthood at twenty-one years of age and would be introduced to younger children as Uncle or Aunt but to us older children, or 'us kids,' they were still be simply Cousins. Some older children, such as Cousin Clarence who had left school younger than most at thirteen and gone to work on the roads with his father, Uncle Johnny, were often called by a nickname. I doubt that Boof would answer to the name Clarence except by one of his older relatives. Some of my other cousins included Burr Cutter and Sheep Dog who were older teenagers and worked on their farms with their farther and Mixo who seemed to spend most of his time chasing rabbits.

These worthy older boys had not yet achieved the status of Uncle yet, so they were simply referred to by us kids as the 'big boys' and they were generally our role models and heroes, apart from movie types such as Hopalong Cassidy and later John Wayne.

We also had female cousins as well, which was not surprising as country families tended to be large, unlike those in the city who had other things to do like going to the club, or later watching television. Gender did not seem to matter and so younger girls had equal status as cousins and their differences were accepted and they, with their greater ability to tolerate obnoxious boys, did the same. Some considerations were assumed by both genders as implicit; there would be no kissing and skinny dipping in the farm dam was purely a boy thing. Most of the female cousins who were in our little group of 'us kids' generally got involved with group exercises such as climbing trees, playing cricket and generally roaming freely about. Unfortunately, this freedom and equity was often spoilt when they became older teenagers and started to see that such habits as wearing dresses, doing their hair nicely and generally looking well-scrubbed were useful in attracting a serious boyfriend. When this happened, they became another class of cousin which required more formal rules such as not sneaking up on them when they were sitting in the haystack with their current boyfriend or referring publicly to some unfortunate habit which they had as a youngster.

They were in that uncomfortable period of cousinship which precluded all of the fun activities such as billycart racing, mud fights and adventures such as exploring the darkened, tree lined billabong up the creek or the haunted house which had long since fallen into disrepair on the edge of town. A few girls who seemed to be have avoided becoming a little princess went on to achieve status amongst the 'big boy' set. These girls, like cousin Gemina, who lived well out of town on her parent's sheep station called Blackwater, were accepted into this senior group and were a great influence in controlling some of the more restless boys amongst them. Boof in particular was in awe of cousin Gemina who could ride a horse like the best of them and was known to be a crack shot with a rifle. She was also a smart girl with a good practical sense who would no doubt go on to be a good farmer's wife who would stick with her husband and family through the usual bush seasons of fire, flood, drought and pestilence; the usual problems which sometimes cropped up in this part of the country.

There were some in our little group who obviously were not related and so we called them by their nickname or their first name which usually was changed to suit the degree of friendship. So, I became Tommo, Andrew who lived on the edge of town was Andy and so on. Names were important social labels, so such monikers as Clarence were soon replaced in the gang by some term of affection such as Boof, regardless of its other connotations.

Sometimes it is often forgotten by the younger generation of city dwellers that Australia in the 1950's was still very much a young country. It had only broken away as a colony of Great Britain fifty years ago and there were still many people who still considered themselves as British. In fact, the country still had God Save the King as its national anthem and there were places further inland where no white man had yet walked. Gemina's father and brothers, and I suspect she also, still went wild pig hunting on horseback with hand guns.

This year was the town's 120th anniversary and as a form of dubious celebration, some of the local graziers drove a large mob of sheep right through the town and down its wide main street, Comur Street, which seemed to be ideal for that purpose and if fact had been built that way. It was a most spectacular sight for a city kid to watch such a large number of animals being driven down the main street with drovers on their stock horses cracking long whips and keeping their flock from climbing up onto the boardwalks where we were standing and into open shop doors. It was a great spectacle but had little historical significance because the railhead on the main line did not open until the 1880's some sixty years after the first development of the town. Well, I guess that the sheep in those days had to be driven somewhere, even just to the local abattoir.

Nanna and all of her many relatives, including my mother who had been born in the town in 1909, easily fitted into this type of celebration because their families had been there at the beginning anyway. My mother had been one of nine children, although three of them had died in infancy; a common thing in those days. She was the only surviving girl in a group of brothers who had moved into the city with the family, the Rawsons, during the Great Depression. Her father, George Rawson had been born in Yass in the 1870's and was the town's blacksmith, farrier and general carrier. His father, Thomas had been born on a sheep station further to the southeast near the then new township of Queanbeyan and had moved over to Yass and had set up the blacksmith shop there. It was George's father, William Rawson who had migrated from Bishopstone, Wiltshire in England with his young family on the emigrant ship the *Woodbridge* which had arrived in the colonies in 1838. He and his pregnant wife Anne had left the hardship and starvation of their English village to come across to the other side of the world and start a new life. Her son James had been born on the ship, and, after a short time of adjustment in Sydney Town, William had bought a small horse and cart to carry his young family, their meagre possessions and the few blacksmith's tools which he was able to take from England, and headed off to the new country opening up around Queanbeyan. They had six more children but later moved to Yass only fifty miles to the northwest where there was better land. The family had extended further with marriages to local farmers and towns people and so by now, it seemed that most of the local population were related in some form or other to Nanna and to Mum and I. Belonging to a large, caring group of people who would cheerily wish you 'good day' on sight and called you by name was a great feature of the happy, country life which I was now experiencing.

The Revenge of the Bunyip

Saturday nights were usually special at Nanna's house. There would always be a crowd of people coming to visit. Uncle Johnny, Nanna's son and Boof her grandson, would come early in the evening for dinner. Before it got dark, Uncle Johnny would cut some timber for the wood heap and generally do some of the little necessities of maintenance around the house whilst Boof would go and talk to his grandfather in the front bedroom. They got on well, did Uncle Stan and Boof. Poor Uncle Stan was not up for long and deep discussions and these were equally beyond Boof. They talked about horses mainly, Uncle Stan's passion and the form of various nags in the upcoming Picnic Races.

Dinner was a very informal affair on those nights with Uncle Johnny, Nanna and Mum sitting on one side of the big, scrubbed pine table and Boof and I at the ends. I had forgotten to mention that the table was pressed up hard against the wall and usually was the repository or various sundry items needing attention, such as shopping bags, and lists of groceries, letters and other items of mail requiring attention, all sorts of paraphernalia for knitting and sewing, including work clothes that Uncle Johnny always seemed to bring home on many occasions. However, sometime before setting the table, these items were usually cleared out of the way, often into one of the comfortable old lounge chairs which were never used in the front parlour.

The delicious food would be served up, usually some sort of meat stew with potatoes and carrots and beans, and the eating and conversation would begin. Boof seemed to have missed the lesson, given many a time by Nanna, about talking with one's mouth full and so his eating habits reminded me of those tumble dryers I had seen in the new coin laundry back in the shopping centre near home. Poor Nanna! She had long since given up with teaching Boof some manners, but at least he did try – on occasions, dinner not being one of them.

After dinner, Nanna and Mum would clear the table and Uncle Johnny would go out onto the bench on the front veranda for a smoke. Boof would go into the front parlour to clear the large, round rosewood table which was the centre piece of that room and cover it with a green, felt tablecloth. In winter, he would light a fire in the open fireplace and rearrange the chairs, taking some from the kitchen as well. Saturday night, I soon found, was card night and many of Nanna's relatives and some friends would come over to play poker or some other card game. It was more of a social event than a gambling spree; the players would often play for match sticks or even pennies if Uncle Errol came. Now here was a man with a gambling habit; he would bet on two cockroaches climbing up a wall if there was someone silly enough to take the bet. Nanna hinted that he 'kept a book' at the local pub, whatever that meant!

On my first night of this family gathering, Uncle Johnny gave me a wink and said:

"Come on, young Thomas. Let me show you a family secret."

I was most interested in what this might be, so I got up from the dinner table and followed my second cousin out of the back door and down the little track which led to the outhouse. He went past it for a short distance and then stopped. Here was that large circular ring of stones covered with old sheets of corrugated iron, mostly rusted in parts, and logs to keep them lifting off in the wind, which I had often passed on my many explorations down to the creek.

On second glance, I realised that the circle of stones was actually a low wall and as Uncle Johnny began to slide back some of the iron sheets that this mysterious structure was actually a water well. I peered down over his bent shoulder into a deep and dark circular pit lined with stone. Not far down was a black pool of water.

Uncle Johnny stood up and reached for a long rope which I had just noticed ran down the closest wall of the well and into the dark water below. He began hauling on the rope and soon a rather shapeless mass of hessian slowly emerged from the water. It was a bag which made a strange clinking sound as he pulled it up the side of the well. Having landed his catch on the ground next to the well, he untied a strong leather cord which was threaded around the lip of the bag and extracted several large brown beer bottles.

"This will do for a while, "he said and retied the bag and lowered it carefully back into the well. Sliding back the sheets of iron, he gave me another wink and returned to the house. So, this was the family secret; well, at least one of them anyway. Back in the kitchen, he opened one of the bottles and poured a little into a glass tumbler and handed it to me. He also poured a generous amount into another class and said:

"Cheers, mate!"

Now it was not uncommon at home for my mother to give me a little glass of beer when my uncles came over, so having a small glass with Uncle Johnny was not a novelty. Actually, at home, my mother would often give me a glass of deep, black stout in the hope that this rich liquid would 'put a little meat' on my skinny frame.

This beer was the coldest that I have ever tasted and my front teeth ached something terrible. Uncle Johnny also proudly boasted that the tasty beer was one of his own brewing, something which he did often using two honey cans which were used to swap over the ingredients from time to time. The old well had long since been used as a source of drinking water. Now it was used for another purpose for drinking and I doubt that any refrigerator in the city could do as well as that old stone well.

The sun had now set and back in the house as the other guests had started to arrive. In those days, when people visited on such an occasion as this, the entire family would also go. The adults would stay in the front parlour and the children would go straight to the kitchen and the friendly glow and warmth of the fuel stove. Uncle Stan would sometimes make an effort and come out of the front bedroom, walking painfully with his walking stick, and be seated on cushions in a large rocking chair closest to the open fire. He was close enough to the round table to take a hand at cards and especially a glass of Uncle Johnny's 'medicine' from the well.

Out in the kitchen, the dinner items had been cleared and replaced with small plates of homemade biscuits – shortbread being Nanna's speciality – small cakes and fairy bread. This last item was one of Mum's favourite party foods, it consisted of white bread well covered in butter and sprinkled with those little coloured balls of candy which we called hundreds and thousands. These slices were very popular with us kids and given a chance, few remained after the first assault. Luckily, there was always an extra supply kept in a cake tin outside in the Coolgardie Safe. There were also several large bottles of soft drink – lemonade and creaming soda mostly – which Uncle Johnny had brought in a big box earlier that evening. Of course, it also contained some replacement bottles for the well outside.

As all of the chairs had been taken from the kitchen into the front room, Nanna had spread a huge blanket onto the linoleum-covered floor of us to sit on. This was not to be for Boof, as he held supreme as the leader of the 'big boys' who were there, including Cousin Gemina who kept a maternal eye on what we younger kids got up to.

On this night, when all of the adults had settled themselves and their glasses of beer or sherry around the table in the front parlour, Boof turned off the hurricane lamp and left us all in the eerie red glow of the open grate of the fuel stove. The shadows on the wall alone would conjure up some fiery pit of hell. Little Cousin Alice who was all of four years of age cuddled up to Cousin Gemina who was furthest from the fire. Boof did not help matters by jumping up and sitting on the table like Old Nick himself.

Boof was in his element now leering down at the younger children and the older ones who knew what to expect and all grinned expectedly. Boof was now the teller of tales, as he leaned closer down from the table and said in a quiet but mysterious tone:

"Tonight, I'll tell youse of the tale of the Bunyip of Brogan's Pool."

There was a shudder amongst the littlies and a stifled laugh from the oldsters because everyone in the town knew of Brogan's Pool. It was a small but deep pool just up the creek at the back of the house and not far from where we now sat in the fiery darkened room. I found out later that this particular pool had been named after Jonas Brogan, a local Irish identity, something of a swagman, who had drowned in the pool about the time that Uncle Stan as a young man was building this house. Brogan had often camped by the pool and sometimes had come up to the house to 'cadge' some tea or sugar following the long tradition of such itinerant workers who wandered from town to town and from farm to farm looking for work – and of course some free supplies. Apparently, he had own supplies of Ishka Baha or 'the hard stuff' as Uncle Stan would call whiskey, and one night had finished off the bottle, gone too close to the edge of the muddy bank and had slipped in. He didn't come out until the next day when a local lad reported indignantly to the police that there was a body floating in his favourite fishing spot. It was considered a sad event by the local people who had a soft spot for old Paddy Brogan but local kids really knew what had dragged him into the cold, black water.

Mothers, my own being included, had often warned their youngsters not to go to the muddy banks of Brogan's Pool as it was dangerous. When curious kids asked why, they were often told very sharply that they just shouldn't do so, or if the parent was a little more forthcoming simply that they might slip in and drown just like poor Paddy Brogan. Such discussion about this pool had been going on for thousands of years as Boof informed us, having found a small spark of uncommon knowledge, because the local indigenous Ngunnawal people had been saying the same thing for all of that time. Except, he informed us with an evil grin, that their reason was that there was a Bunyip living in the pool which ate children. They probably had their own local name for this Bunyip, that mythical aquatic and carnivorous beast which supposedly inhabited outback rivers, billabongs and pools and featured a lot in stories told to the children of indigenous peoples.

"It's the truth!" said Boof, "because Daddy Ryan told me so and he's an old Ngunnawal man who works with me on the roads and knows everything."

Little Cousin Alice cuddled closer to Cousin Gemina as Boof went on to describe the Bunyip as being about as large as a bull with a great round head prominent ears and whiskers like a seal or otter. They have shaggy black fur, small tusks, and an elongated, maned neck and a horse-like tail. Bunyips, according to Boof can swim swiftly with fins or flippers, have a loud, roaring call:

"Rrrrurr, rrrrurr, whoosh, "Rrrrurr, rrrrurr, whoosh" Boof called out loudly in a deep voice, giving his version of the sound of the Bunyip. The youngsters all cowed as Boof swept his hand across the little group on the floor. The older boys again stifled a laugh and little Cousin Alice began to cry.

Now, with a few glasses of lemonade in them, there were thoughts in some young minds of going to the toilet. This was absolutely the very last option for the younger children and even some of the older boys who had taken some of Boof's dramatic explanations to heart.

Going to the outhouse at night had always been a problem with me living here at Auchenblae; my only concern with this gentle way of life. There was a Chamber Pot below our big, four-poster bed in the spare bedroom but to me, as a city kid this was also not much of an option. If I was 'caught short' in the night, I would hang on for as long as I could until I finally felt that I was going to disgrace myself in our shared bed. Then I would wake up my poor mother and ask her to take me to the toilet. Mothers take such unpleasant chores as simply being part of being a mother and so she would light the bedside candle, put on her gown and slippers and take her grateful little boy off to the toilet. It was always cold and dark out there and even at my age, I wondered what creatures lurked in the darkness. Certainly, there were snakes but Mum assured me that if we made lots of noise and trod heavily, they would keep to the long grass. It was usually only in the daytime when they lay on the track to get warm that one had to watch out. When asked about what happened when the toilet can was full – boys tended to ask such questions at strange times of day or night – my mother would simply laugh and tell me that the Night Man would come and carry it away to his cart and replace it with an empty one. For many years I thought that this worthy person was mythical – someone like the tooth fairy or those other useful house elves, about which my teachers at school read from books by the Brothers Grimm. Eventually I saw such a person emptying the sewerage cans into his rather smelly tanker truck and my clean childhood fantasy vanished along with the sludge going into the truck.

Cousin Boof had finished his story about the Bunyip of Bogan's Pond and leaned back to down another glass of creaming soda. Little Cousin Alice had buried herself into the coat of Cousin Gemina and some of the other younger children were looking about with some apprehension thinking whether or not their need to go to the toilet was worth being taken by the Bunyip. It could have easily slithered down the creek hearing young voices to near where the dunny now stood. Seeing their distress and getting a little joy from his impact on the youngsters, Boof now proudly boasted in a casual way that he was not afraid of any such creature and was going out for a short 'wee break'. With that, he got up, lit the small candle which had stood dark on the table, dramatically threw open the back door and went out into Bunyip territory.

It was just then that Uncle Errol came in from the front parlour to go out to get some more supplies from the well and saw little Cousin Alice crying. He asked Cousin Gemina what was wrong and she exclaimed:

"Aw! Silly Cousin Boof scared the wits out of 'er wif a story abawt the Bunyip an' he's gorn oht to tha dunny an' left tha door open."

"Oh, has he?" said Uncle Errol, a wicked gleam in his eye as he gave the older boys a wink. He reminded me of the British actor Terry Thomas whom I had seen at the movies; he had the same slicked back dark hair parted in the middle and a thin black moustache. I thought that at any moment he would twist one end of the said moustache before suggesting something wicked. Instead, he turned about and went back into the front parlour.

It was only a few minutes later when we heard that dreaded noise in the distance out beyond the safety of the house:

"Rrrrurr, rrrrurr, whoosh, "Rrrrurr, rrrrurr, whoosh".

Suddenly and with an expression of great fear on his face, Boof rushed into the kitchen and slammed the back door shut, leaning back on it just to add some meagre security. He still had one hand holding up his undone trousers and was visibly shaken. The younger children simply stared and felt sure that there would be a Bunyip just outside the door. The older boys just smirked at each other as they guessed what had happened. Later I was told the story by my mother and Nanna in between fits of laughter.

Uncle Errol, always the lad himself, had quickly sized up the situation and had decided then and there to pay some of Boof's terrorism back. He had gone back into the front parlour where Nanna kept a great range of curiosities and artifacts given to her and Uncle Stan over the many years. One of them was a bullroarer, a carved and flattened wooden stick about ten inches long attached to a long coil of leather thread. It had been given to Uncle Stan by a Ngunnawal man who he had helped back in the old days. Such devices, when whirled around the head gave a deep, growling sound:

"Rrrrurr, rrrrurr, whoosh, "Rrrrurr, rrrrurr, whoosh".

Was the sound it made and it was used in some of the secret men's ceremonies of the tribe.

Uncle Errol had long since been fascinated by such artefacts and had played with it as a boy out the front of the house. He knew where it lay on the sideboard in the front parlour along with the blue carved emu egg and the carved boomerang. Taking it up and giving another leering wink to the adults, he had slipped out of the front door and around the side of the house. There was another small track going down to the creek past the old stables which Uncle Stan would walk to fetch water for his old horse. This bypassed the outhouse where a small glimmer of light showed that Boof was enthroned.

Creeping up from the direction of the creek, the typical route that any self-respecting, child-eating Bunyip would take, he stood up and whirled the bullroarer around his head:

"Rrrrurr, rrrrurr, whoosh, "Rrrrurr, rrrrurr, whoosh".

"Rrrrurr, rrrrurr, whoosh, "Rrrrurr, rrrrurr, whoosh", went the bullroarer. The door of the outhouse burst open and a terrified Boof came screaming up the track to the house, his pants still about his knees and a flurry of newspaper left in his wake.

The revenge of the Bunyip had been taken.

The Yabbies are Biting

There weren't many houses along the Good Hope Road; in fact, there were only two as far as I could see near Auchenblae. The closest was just a few yards up the road from us and on the other side of the road. It was owned by the Cholmondeley family, Jim and his wife Esme. They had a son about my age called Jim junior, but because he pronounced his surname as Chumlee and hated being called Junior, we kids just called him Chums.

Now the Cholmondeley's farm was very much like Auchenblae; small and generally neglected. Uncle Johnny, who was a drinking mate of Jim Cholmondeley down at the Commercial said that he had come from England many years ago and worked in the city. He was simply called Pommie or Pom by his mates - that coverall name for anyone coming from the old country. Pom had a romantic idea of farming, so after he was married, he took his new wife and young son and moved out to the country. He bought this small property because it was all he could afford and it was about the same size as those with which he was familiar in the Old Dart.

The only trouble with Pom was that he was not a farmer, just an ex-bank city insurance salesman who thought that anybody could farm a small piece of land. Wrong! He had been quite pleased with himself when he was able to purchase a small farm out along the Good Hope Road which had black, basalt soil – good farming land to his way of thinking. The first thing that he found out when he arrived, was that his little few acres was cheap because it was also full of small rocks, mainly of rounded undecomposed basalt.

Uncle Johnny and his mates would joke about this with him, calling him a 'rock farmer' and asking him how his crop was going. He had also bought a cheap, second-hand tractor and plough from McWhirter's, the local Stock and Station agent, but seemed to be always going back to the store to buy new blades for his plough. It seemed that Pom spend most of his time hand harvesting these rocks which were generally about a foot across and rounded. He would pile them up into a small trailer hooked up to the back of the tractor and then dump them close to the house. Being a man whose optimism far exceeded his knowledge of farming, he decided to do something with the great pile of small boulders which now had grown to a considerable height next to the house. So he started building stone walls which would be most useful, he thought in fencing off his land. This was a constant source of interest to all and sundry who drove past his farm.

Eventually, he had enough ploughed land to plant corn and was very proud when his paddocks sprouted green shoots. Then the drought came and there was no rain for five years. The green shoots withered and died and those which remained were quickly eaten by the locust plague which always seemed to follow the hot, dry weather. Soon, Pom's paddocks were again bare soil except for a new crop of boulders which had sprung up when the dry topsoil was blown away. Farming can be a hard life and so in the end, he sold his little tractor and plough and took a job in the town, working at McWhirter's, the local Stock and Station agent as an insurance salesman.

With time and the end of the drought, the land once more looked green and grass once more grew on Pom's little farm and his dam once more filled with water. As city kid, I always thought that the term dam was rather grandiose for these small, often shallow, round scraped hollows which dotted the countryside in places which would catch surface runoff. To my limited experience, a dam was something huge which held vast amounts of water, such as the great Warragamba Dam which was then being built west of Sydney, or the Burrinjuck Dam which Mum had told me about. This was further down the Yass Valley and she had said that her father had had something to do with carting supplies to its construction site. Never-the-less, every good farm would have its dam and we kids would be warned by our mothers not to go too close or we might fall in and drown. Such things seemed to happen on occasions.

These warnings went by the board as young Chum and I would regularly go down to his dam to launch one of the rafts we had made out of old kerosene drums and planks; drowning was for other kids and swagmen of folk legend. But dams had other uses too.

It was when we were launching our latest craft, with the help of Black Bob, one of our cronies who was a good mate of Boof, and brother of Cousin Gemina. He came from Blackwater Station which was a few miles out of town, but on the weekends, Gemina and her brother would often come into town with their parents. More often than not, they would walk out to Nanna's place to stay overnight to play and enjoy her home cooked meals. Cousin William was called Black Bob because he came from Blackwater and because he was a pessimist's pessimist. Nothing in the world had the potential for going right, according to Black Bob, whom we simply called Bob or Blackie. He did not mind this latter epithet as it was part of belonging to the group to have a nickname – the more obscure the better.

"Aww! I don't think she'll float' was the first thing Blackie said when he saw our latest craft of four empty kerosene drums lashed to several boards by rope. But Chum and I just smiled and together the three of us carried the raft down to the dam.

"Ya need a rope attached to it to pull it out when she sinks," was Blackie's next helpful suggestion.

Our raft floated high and dry and soon the three of us were paddling our craft across the muddy waters of the dam. It was a sunny day and it was great just to lie on our raft and watch the clouds wander past overhead.

As we paddled our craft back to shore using our fence paling paddles, Blackie pointed up to one of the steep earth banks and pointed out some holes which were not far from the waterline.

"Ya got yabbies here. Look at them old holes in the bank! You know that they bury themselves in the mud when there's a big dry and then come out when it rains? But they probably are all dead by now." he said mournfully.

"No, they're not!" exclaimed Chum looking intensely at the bubbles rising up from the depths of the dam. "Look! These are yabby bubbles!

Sure enough, there were several small streams of bubbles breaking the surface near the bank. "Let's go yabby fishing," he said excitedly. This was yet another new type of adventure to me and Chum had to explain to me that a yabby was a small, freshwater crayfish – thing like a prawn – which also made good eating. Now I was used to the prawns that Mum brought home at Christmas and so I could understand his excitement.

Later, after a little childish persuasion, Chum had convinced his mother that we should go yabby fishing that night; yabbies being nocturnal and shy creatures. His mother was only convinced when Chum had explained that we would have Cousin Gemina, a reliable older girl, to look after our well-being during the expedition. All we needed to do was to ask Cousin Gemina and my mother.

Cousin Gemina reluctantly agreed to chaperone the yabby fishers, but only after Blackie promised to do her chores on the farm for the next week. "It'll probably kill me," whined Bob but he agreed.

Yabby fishing is considered a traditional sport out in the country and there are many schools of thought as to how they should be caught. This was often the topic of many a lunchtime debate at the local school I was told and often caused many a playground scuffle. One school of thought favoured a passive approach for maximum efficiency and numbers caught. This involved the use of a yabby trap made out of fine mesh with a funnel-like entrance into which the yabbies would go but not be able to return. The trap would be baited with some form of bloody meat, rotten vegetables such as pumpkin or even cakes of raw soap. Others favoured a more sporting approach. This would involve the construction of yabby poles made from a long, flexible stick such as willow, with a long length of string attached to one end. The bait, usually meat in this method, would be strongly tied at the other end of the string for the yabby to latch onto with its big claws. Even here, there were differences of opinion as to how the yabby should be landed. The cautious approach was to very slowly pull the string in once a sudden pull on the string had indicated that a yabby was now trying to pull the meat off. A more sporting approach was to suddenly flick the yabby out of the water with a strong overhead sweep of the pole before the yabby could let go. The hapless creature would then be carefully picked up and placed in a bucket of water until sufficient were caught. It was this last method that Blackie now suggested and we spent some time making our poles from willow branches down near the creek at the back of Nanna's house. String was available in any amount in most homes in the country so that was no problem. Mum had reluctantly agreed to my night expedition because she thought that I should experience some of the skills which she had learned as a young girl. She cut up some sausages which Nanna was keeping in the safe on the back veranda for bait; Blackie suggested that this would not be good enough and that we would not catch anything with sausages. He suggested freshly-killed rabbit, but this type of meat was not immediately available so we had to settle for sausage meat. We hoped that the yabbies would too.

So it was, that later in the evening after dinner, Blackie, Gemina and I wandered down the road in the faint glow of a small kerosene lantern over to Chum's house. He was ready and his mother had prepared a small basket of home-made cakes and a large bottle of lemonade with some cups. It was easier to continue down the road as there was a considerable amount of high grass between the house and the dam and our destination was not far inside the property anyway. We had no worries about traffic at that hour of night as vehicles seldom went down the Good Hope road at that hour – or any hour for that matter.

We climbed through the double strand barbed wire of the fence, Gemina holding up the top strand with one hand and pushing down on the other with her boot. No prim and proper shoes for Cousin Gemina! She was a country girl off the farm and so jeans, checked shirt and boots were her usual attire. Gum boots for this particular evening. We pushed through the long grass towards the dam.

"Damn!" said Blackie who was wearing only sandshoes and had trodden in a small trickle of water which flowed down from the dam.

We walked quietly around the bare edge of the dam, with Gemina trying to hold the lantern so that it would not shine onto the water and scare our quarry. We found a dry patch of grass near the edge of the dam and settled down to get ready for catching our prey.

The three of us sat on the edge of the dam and tossed our sausage-baited lines in. Chum was right about one thing; the dam was well stocked with yabbies as we soon were getting strong tugs on our lines. Chum and I both opted for the slow haul method but I, being the novice, soon lost mine and pulled in an empty line. No matter! There was some spare sausage meat in a bag which Nanna had given me; she had long equipped yabby expeditions.

Chum was more experienced or luckier than I and pulled in a nice big yabby about six inches long. A light blue beauty with many legs and big nippers. Blackie had decided in the sporting approach and was regularly flicking his line overhead with the idea that the quick response would catch the prey. No luck! If he had any bites on the line, he was too slow in reacting to them and so caught nothing.

"I told you it was going to be a waste of time," he said moaning and got up and went a few steps behind us to take off his wet shoes and socks.

Cousin Gemina was now hauling yabbies in at a good rate; she was the undisputed expert in this field and soon we had quite a few in our bucket of water. Gemina explained that one should not overfill the bucket, as yabbies were good climbers and would soon get out. Only a few inches in the bottom were enough and when there were enough yabbies, we would take them back to Nanna's where she would cook them to a lovely red colour by dropping them into boiling water for a couple of minutes. I thought that this was not terribly humane, but then again, I was new to country survival and was quite happy to buy tins of tuna and other processed meat back home. Prawns, crayfish and now yabbies were not to my liking as I believed, in my very limited taste experience of lamb or beef and three veg, that anything with more than four legs was rather suspect as a food source.

Any form of fishing for me, including my new experience of yabby fishing, was usually just a distraction for what was going on around me. I had been out fishing with one of my uncles and his son on Sydney Harbour but did not share their love of angling. I was happy just to muck around in boats and watch all of the other traffic on the water and the beautiful harbour all around. Tonight, my distraction was the night sky.

Sydney was not a good place to look at the stars; there was too much pollution; and this was in the days when the word pollution was rarely mentioned by anyone, including the press. The mills and factories in Botany, not far from my home at the Junction, simply put all of their smoke, fumes and noxious gases up into the air. Mum used to complain, to herself mainly, about the black soot from the local coal-fired power station at Bunnerong a few miles away. This black dust usually came down on washing day when there was a southerly wind, and my poor mother would have to rewash all of the clothes and sheets and hang them out again when the wind changed. Besides, there was always a sea breeze, as Mum would call it blowing in from the ocean just a few miles away to our east. This was a regular event due to the south-easterly winds which were the most prevalent winds in this part of the world. The neighbours were always complaining that it rusted their tools and pushbikes. Luckily cars were not common in our street, otherwise they would have rusted too.

My mates and I in Sydney would often explore far and wide on our own pushbikes which were slowly rusting, and we would often ride past the car factory at Pagewood a few miles further west. Its chimneys would be belching out great brown fumes which I later found out would dissolve in rain to make a strong acid which fell on the newly-made cars in the huge holding yard just below the chimneys. These vehicles then had a good start in their own rusting process even before they were sold.

Tonight however, there was no air pollution out here in the country and the clouds had cleared away. The sky was filled with a great, sparkling mass of brilliant stars. It was then that I realised that they varied in brightness and colour. Cousin Gemina who was going to the high school and liked to study such things noticed my interest, or at least my head held up looking at the sky, eyes wide and mouth open.

"That's Beetlejuice!" she said pointing up at a group of stars looking like a saucepan and containing the said mentioned red star. I thought that its name was rather strange but then again, I knew nothing of astronomy at that stage. Occasionally there would be a quick streak of faint light in the sky which Cousin Gemina said was a 'shooting star' and that when we saw one, we should make a wish. I wondered what the connection was between such a sighting and wishing for something, but then again astrology was not my strong point either. Blackie just sat in the darkness rubbing his wet toes and bemoaning the fact that it would probably be raining by midnight.

I went back to give my yabby angling a second chance and decided to follow Blackie's method of the fast flick. I tried this several times when I had some nibbles on my line but nothing came out except a wet piece of sausage on a wetter string which hit Blackie in the face.

"Watch it!" he said indignantly and so I shortened the string and went back for another try. Suddenly there was a very strong pull on my line; the biggest that I had all evening. I waited a bit hoping that the yabby at the other end was a big one with huge claws which would now be grasping the delicious sausage meat. Now! I quickly flicked my line out of the water and had a faint impression of something large flying over my head.

"Ooohw!" came a pitiful cry from behind me. Cousin Gemina dropped her line and picked up the lamp to see what had caused the fuss.

In the faint lamplight, there was Blackie struggling to pull a huge yabby off his foot where it had attached itself firmly to his big toe by one of its great claws.

"Get it orf me!" cried the stricken Blackie.

Cousin Gemina reached up and grabbed her panicked brother by the foot and the yabby just behind its head. With a light squeeze of its body, she pulled the creature from Blackie's toe and tossed the king of all yabbies into the bucket. Blackie just grabbed his painful toe and cursed crayfish of all varieties in words that a young boy should not know. The yabbies were certainly biting that night.

A Trip into Town

Life at Auchenblae was not confined to the little cottage on the Good Hope Road; far from it! Nana was a very outgoing person and well-known in the district, being a descendent of several of the pioneering families who had settled there more than a hundred years ago. She would often set up Uncle Stan for the morning with breakfast and his newspaper and then go visiting into town.

I remember well the first time that she took Mum and me into town. It was exciting for both of us; for Mum it was a time to revisit the town in which she grew up and for me a great adventure into the world of the country township.

It was only about a mile into town and walking was the way of things in those days. Few people owned a motorcar, even in our street back in the big city. Mr. Thompkins who lived two doors down from us on our little street had a ute because he was a 'tradie' and needed to carry stuff to work and the Hobsons who were particularly good friends of Mum had a motorbike with sidecar. It always was a great thrill to hear that old motor bike coming down our street in the late afternoon.

On that particular day, the day of my first walk into town, Mum had dressed herself in her best holiday dress and shoes and helped me put on the little khaki safari suit and sun hat which she dressed me in for special occasions Nanna wrote out a shopping list, picked up her broad, shopping basket and said goodbye to Uncle Stan. Out the door, down the flagstone path, through the old wooden gate between the two tall poplar trees and turn left to head off along the narrow, dirt path which ran next to the road. Into town.

Soon we had passed the last of the old farm's overgrown paddock with its crop of tall, brown grass and thistles, and onto the main bitumen road which joined Yass to the little town of Murrumbateman to the south. Being an important road at the outskirts of the town, our little dirt track had matured into a proper, cement footpath. There were also other people using the path and I was impressed by the number of men who raised their hats as they passed, usually with a 'Good Morning, Mrs. McLaren'. The woman we passed almost always gave the same greeting except for a few of the younger ones who must have known her well as children who addressed her simply but with respect as Nanna. Hanna McLaren was certainly well-known and loved in the district.

It had only been about a mile into town along that little dusty track by the side of the road which ran south towards Good Hope. That was nothing for country women like Mum and Nanna. I was content with looking at all of the new sights and sounds of the country; even the old paddock which was owned by Uncle Stan and now, like its owner had seen better times. It was covered in tall, dry brown grass and purple-capped Scottish thistles; not a pleasant place for a casual stroll but still interesting in its own right.

Mum and Nanna discussed all sorts of things along the way, mainly what Mum's relations had been up to since she left all of those years ago. Most of them lived in the town but some had moved out to own or work on outlying properties; which grew mainly wheat or grazed sheep. There was a suggestion by Nanna's silence that a few had gone away to the war and had not returned. Australia had suffered a lot during those times.

Finally, we reached the main street of Yass which was signed as Comur Street, which seemed to extend as a broad tree-lined avenue as far as I could see. The buildings were mainly two-story or single houses on its outskirts. No high rise here! We crossed over to the other side of the road and stepped up onto the footpath which was bitumen tarred. With a few exceptions, the buildings had a continuous row of over-hanging awnings on the front which sheltered the pedestrians from rain – when it finally came. The exceptions were the imposing commercial buildings such as banks and the imposing Post Office with its tall clock tower. They were on the western side of the street, possibly to keep its patrons and staff from the intense heat of the afternoon sun.

We walked along, Nanna, Mum and me holding her hand. I found every shop and building of great interest. There were some similarities to my suburb at home but very few. At home in the Junction, the main shops lacked awnings and were clustered around the main intersection as though they needed protection from the expanding march of suburbia. Back home, the long and wide expanse of ANZAC Parade, which ran from the City to Botany Bay, ran through the shopping centre where it crossed Maroubra Road forming the well-known junction.

Down the centre of the Parade in its own nature strip ran the tram lines with their bustling little trams carrying people to and from the city. The other broad street which formed the Junction, Maroubra Road, was where some trams turned and headed east up and over the big hill, and on to the beach. Other trams continued along the Parade south and eventually came to La Perouse, that distant and mysterious suburb on the shores of Botany Bay.

Well, it was mysterious to my friends and I who would often catch the tram there for a morning of excitement. There was a large indigenous community there and their elders would often put on a show with boomerang throwing and tales of their Dreamtime. There was also Ram Chandra, the Indian Snake Man. He would put on a show for all of the tourists who would come and stand around the small, corrugated iron fence of his enclosure whilst he would extract various snakes, mostly poisonous ones such as the brown snake and taipan and handle them (carefully) to show their features off to the astounded public. On wild days, when the Southerly Buster blew huge waves through the heads of Botany Bay, my friends and I would take the small, wooden ferry across to Kurnell, the place where Cook first landed in 1770. That would be an exciting ride as the brave little ferry jumped this way and that as it pushed its snub nose through the waves. We often found that our ferry ride 'on the high seas' as we fantasised, was usually the last for the day, being cancelled on the return trip home due to the rough weather.

Back in Yass, Nanna went about her usual shopping chores with Mum helping to remind her of the various small items which we would need. Nanna also carried a large 'string bag', a woven net-like oval bag with two big cane handles in her shopping basket. Uncle Stan had made these many years ago before he became bed-ridden. Mum told me how he and Nanna would sit in front of the warm kitchen stove of an evening and weave these bags in much the same way as fishermen made fishing nets, using a long, broad wooden netting needle and a wooden frame. Nanna still made some of these for her relatives when they were needed; there were no disposable plastic bags and other wasteful containers in those days.

Into each shop we would go. There was Lombardi's fruit and vegetable shop with its sign saying in big letters and very fine print:

CREDIT AVAILABLE
But only to those over 80 and they must
be accompanied by their Grandmother.'

It took me a while to fathom the true meaning of this caveat but Mr. Lombardi was a jovial character who always had a nice piece of fruit ready for the children of his customers. Nana told Mum very quietly as they left his shop with a pound of potatoes and some oranges that Mr. Lombardi had been an 'Eyetalian' prisoner-of-war in a camp not too far away but had liked the country so much he stayed and brought his family over in the wave of immigrants which came to the country from Europe after the war.

There was the PDF store on the corner. These initials I was told stood for Produce and Dried Foods and was similar to the greengrocer's shop back home. There, the greengrocer's store had a long counter which ran around two or three sides of the shop. In this PDF store however, there was simply one long counter along one side of the shop, to the left of the big double door as we entered. On the other side facing the counter was a long row of big wooden bins. These had large, hinged lids which could be lifted up and each lid had an ornately-lettered plaque which announced its contents. There were bins for oats, wheat, corn kernels, powdered milk, rice, beans (of various types), nuts, dried fruits such as raisons, flour and a whole host of things which I had never heard of. Other items such as sugar and tea were usually purchased from behind the counter in tins, bags or packets and some cold items such as butter would be brought from the cold room which was through a door at the far end of the shop.

Nanna brought out a shiny Quart Pot[3] from her shopping basket. This was what we called a billy can, it was very shiny with a matching top and wire handle. Nanna went over to the bin labelled Powdered Milk and used the scoop which was tied to the lid by a light rope, to fill the billy. She put the lid of the billy on and gave it a hard tap just to be sure that it was closed. Then she took it over to the other side of the shop to the long, worn wooden counter behind which stood a thin smiling man in a grey dust coat.

---

[3] One Quart = 2 pints and 4 Quarts = 1 gallon. A pint was about 600 millilitres.

"Good morning, Mrs. McLaren. And what can we do for you today?"

Nana put the billy can up onto the grey wooden top and replied:

"Just some powdered milk, today Henry. Oh, and I'll have a couple of tins of peas as well, thank you."

Henry smiled and quickly turned and walked down his side of the counter, where the walls were covered in box-like wooden shelves full of all sorts of canned and bagged items. He moved a little ladder which was on a small trolley rail which ran the length of these shelves and climbed up to where the box of canned peas were regimentally stacked and brought two cans down.

"Here you are, Mrs. McLaren. Is there anything else?" he asked, extracting a pencil from behind his ear to do some calculations on a pad of blank paper clipped to the top of the counter.

"That will be three shillings and sixpence, please," he said. "Do you want that on the slate?"

I had no idea what he meant by the slate. I had heard once at school our teacher saying that in the olden days, children used chalk to write on slates – wooden framed rectangles of a flat, hard, dark grey stone.

When Nanna smiled, nodded her head and thanked Henry for that courtesy, he folded up the paper receipt and put into a small metal cylinder attached to a long wire. He pressed a spring-loaded handle and the little rocket sped up to a small mezzanine floor which I had only just noticed above the door. Here, an elderly lady sat at a small desk on which was a large, silver cash register. She took the paper from its canister giving a little wave and a smile down to Nanna. She would enter the date, goods and amount in her ledger of regular customers so that Nanna could pay at the end of the month – if not at another time later on. Financial transactions were usually casual but honest in these parts. Few people failed to pay their debts after the tough times had passed.

Into Smith's Butcher Shop. This was similar to the one back home with its long glass and shiny grey marble counter along one side of the shop and posters of fat cattle and sheep along the wall on the other.

"Gidday, Mrs. McLaren. What's it fur today?" Burt Smith the butcher would say in his long drawl. He was a short, fat man with a broad, smiling florid face in a round head upon which sat a straw boater hat pushed right to the back. He wore a white shirt with a blue bow tie under an almost white apron – except for the occasional suspicious brown stains.

In the glassed section of the counter sat various items of cut meat; lamb chops, various cuts of steak, rissoles and other things which brought fear to a little boy's mind such as sheep's brains, kidneys and liver. Ugh! I secretly hoped that Nanna was not going to buy any of that stuff! Behind the counter area, hanging from big metals hooks, which were on a long metal rail running along the back wall, were parts of various carcasses of sheep, legs and ribs of cattle and slabs of bacon. There also long links of processed meats such as beef and pork sausages and different types of salami.

"Just a pound of sausages, please Burt," Nanna said, and with a flourish, Burt expertly selected a certain length of the said hanging item, slipping out a very sharp knife from its wooden sheath attached to his broad leather belt, and cut it off from the rest of the chain. He then placed a small piece of grease-proof paper onto his large white scale and looked at the dial with a squinted eye. I was astounded that the weight shown was almost exactly one pound. Practice makes perfect, I guess! He would carefully fold this bundle up and then place it onto a large pile of clean white butchers' paper which he would then fold up into a compact package. He would seal it with a small strip of sticky tape which he would rip off from its small red container on the counter with a flourish.

Into the Acropolis Milk Bar and Café. Another shop run by hard-working, honest recent immigrants; this time from Greece. Con the owner greeted Nanna at the door:

"Good morning, Mrs. McLaren. The same as usual?" he asked. The 'usual' was a generous pot of freshly brewed tea and a nice sweet Greek pastry made by Con's wife, Sophia.

"Yes, thank you Con. For two please and an American Beauty for the lad," she replied as we sat down in one of the several small booths which ran along one wall of the milk bar. This wall was decorated with a simple, but realistic view of what Mum called the Acropolis which she said was in Athens, a big city in the country of Greece from where Con and his family had come. The booths had partitions which were about waist high and consisted of a central table with bench seats. Across the narrow walkway, the counter, which ran the full length of one wall, were jars of all sorts of delights: boiled sweets, striped and sugary; liquorice strips, black and rubbery; musk sticks pink and sweet-smelling; chewing gum in packets; and a host of other delightful lollies with which a small boy wished he could fill his pockets.

I was interested in what this American Beauty was which Nanna had ordered for me. Very soon, a large silver pot of hot tea, a small silver jug of milk and two plain white cups with saucers arrived on a tray; a silver bowl of white sugar and small bottles of condiments already sat against the wall on the table. In the centre of this tray was a tall glass – the type that milk shakes were once served in – tall, thick glass with ribbed sides. Things American were very popular about this time, especially movies, music and newly-appearing fast foods. The contents of this glass really was an American Beauty – it was filled to the top with all things colourful – ice cream, several coloured jellies, cream and strawberry syrup to cap it all. I had never seen such an elaborate treat! What a beauty!

Before leaving, Nanna also bought two pint bottles of full-cream milk which she carefully placed upright into her large basket leaving her string bag for less fragile items. This was one thing where our home life in the city had an advantage over the country; at home, our milk was delivered every morning by the milkman. He would come down our street very early in the morning in his small van, parking every now and again. He would open its side door and take out his hand crate, a sturdy wire contraption which could carry about six full bottles of milk. Then he would run up the walkway along the side of our house, with a gentle tinkling of the glass bottles in the crate, to our little wooden hatch set in the side of the wall. This he would open and put in the number of bottles requested on a cardboard sign which Mum kept there for just such a purpose. 'Two bottles, please' or 'None today, Thank you' or on special occasions 'Two Bottles of milk and one of cream, please'. The Milkman would then take out the empty glass bottles and put them in the spaces now vacant in his hand crate and back he would run to his little van. At school, at recess time, we all were also given milk which came in small one-third pint bottles. These would be placed on the wooden bench seats outside the classroom by some unseen milkman during morning lessons. Sometimes, during summer, if the crates were placed in the wrong place, the sun would heat up the milk inside and so we would have to drink milk slightly warm or even partly soured. The other disadvantage of these deliveries was the aluminium foil which capped the bottles. Occasionally, clever crows would find that they could pick a neat little hole in the top of the bottles and get some of the milk for themselves. Survival of the fittest!

Our shopping for the essentials over, we left Con's milk bar and crossed Comur Street and went over to the Bottle Shop of the Commercial Hotel. In those days, hotels were a place frequented only by men. It was considered as a man's private domain. The size and prosperity of any town could be measured by the number of hotels or pub's it could support. Usually, they occupied a strategic place on the corners of the main street and mining towns such as

Broken Hill in the state's far west seemed to have one on every corner. Yass had a good share and so was considered a prosperous town. The names of the hotels often showed the clientele which they hoped to attract or some local connection. Names such as the Commercial, the Australian, the Club House were often spoken of in the same revered tones as the Shearers Arms, the Railway, the Imperial and the Overlander.

Pubs closed at 6pm in an attempt to stop excessive drunkenness. Mum always said that this was a farce because beer and spirits could be purchased in large amounts before closing time and then drunk at home. Besides, she said, there were always illegal 'sly grog shops' around – if you knew where they were. Going past any hotel at 6 pm was dangerous, Mum warned. Workers who got off work at 5 pm and arrived at the pub, say at 5:30pm only had half an hour to 'get a skin full'. The pub and the street and gutter in front of the hotel would be full of thirsty, desperate men trying to get into the crowded venue and drunks trying to get out. This cultural event was known back home as the '6pm swill' and not a safe place for a young child. I don't know whether or not this occurred down Comur Street at

6 pm but later, as an adult, I found that licencing hours could be sometimes be more 'relaxed' as the doors would close at 6pm but the well-known clientele would stay inside. In another town well to the northwest where I was posted to teach and was one of these 'respected citizens', this would happen every afternoon and the local Police Sergeant would come in through the back door, have his 'few pints' and then announce 'last drinks' when he had had enough; usually around 8pm at which time all would dutifully leave to stagger off towards home.

Woman were strictly prevented from entering the bar, and lounge which had seats and higher prices, but if they must drink beer, then there was a small 'Ladies' Lounge' tucked discretely and unobtrusively through a small door at the farthest end of the building. Women usually drank at home and going into a pub in the city was not considered socially acceptable and even going into the Bottle Shop to buy lemonade as we were now doing could be considered by any uptight observers as being rather risqué. Many years later in the city, there were protests from some free-thinking young women, mostly from the university, who would chain themselves to the foot rests of selected pubs to achieve some form of bemused acceptance from the resident male inhabitants. Eventually there developed a healthier equality of social drinking.

Of course, beer was the standard drink, especially out in the country. At home, ladies would sip sherry, gin and other spirits as they had done for centuries but publicly only 'foreigners' and 'winos' would touch the juice of the grape. Sometimes it was acceptable for housewives to have a 'glass or two' of beer at home with their menfolk with often a small glass for older children. It would take many more years until a wider drinking palate and an internationally-recognised wine industry would be achieved in this country.

The Bottle Shop was an acceptable place for a lady to enter because it sold a great variety of non-alcoholic beverages as well. Bottles of beer, sherry gin and other versions of the 'hard stuff' would be discretely put into brown paper bags to keep prying eyes away from the purchaser's drinking habits. Of course, everyone knew what would be in those paper bags which gave a cheery clinking sound as the shopping bag waltzed along by the side of its owner.

Today, the purchase in the Bottle Shop of the Commercial was a special treat for me; there being plenty of beer in the big brown bottles in the sacks down the well back at Auchenblae and Nanna had a supply of gin and sherry discretely placed within a big wooden sideboard in the front parlour. Today, Nanna purchased two bottles of a well-known brand of lemonade noted for its effervescence. I really enjoyed a glass of this lemonade because the bubbles when poured into a tall glass would come right up to the top to be sipped with relish. The idea of soft drinks of great variety being sold cans in shops had yet to become the norm and American brands of cola were only just beginning to take over the minds and especially the bodies of young people.

Shopping in those tranquil days seemed to be more of a social event and certainly much more civilised. Items were wrapped in clean paper or put into bags or even billy cans and other privately-owned containers used for such specific purposes. Supermarkets were yet to kill the corner store; pre-wrapped items were yet to take over the shops and plastic was almost unheard of. Almost all of the wrapping, glass bottles and packages were recycled. Glass, for example was often sorted into clear, brown or coloured and then taken to recycling depots. Youth groups such as the Boy Scouts often depended upon bottle collections for some of their income and well-organised 'party animals' usually had 44-gallon (100 L) drums in their BBQ area into which their guests would throw their bottles which were then later recycled for cash for more supplies and parties. Few of these people ever reached into their own pocket to pay for their drinking habit. Back home, after a good day at the beach, my friends and I would search the sand for discarded soft drink bottles which could then be redeemed at the local milk bar. This would provide us with some small amounts of cash for some sweets and then a penny fare back to the Junction on the tram instead of walking all of the way.

Paper too was recycled. Fish and chip shops usually wrapped their food items, especially hot chips, in clean white paper and then recycled newspaper. Later as a local paper boy, who delivered the Sunday newspapers to homes and then sold them outside of the church after Mass, I found that I could then retrace my steps a few days later and pick-up the discarded newspaper from my clientele and then resell them to the owner of the fish and chip shop.

Recycling at its finest! Why is recycling so difficult these days? Probably too much plastic pre-wraps, lack of youthful enterprise or too many electronic distractions!

The morning's tasks completed, Nanna, Mum and I would then walk back along the dusty little track to Auchenblae and store away our purchases; the meat, bottled milk and butter went into the Coolgardie Safe out on the back veranda and the other items in their appropriate metal canisters or on the shelves in the pantry. Nanna would then empty her purse onto the scrubbed top of the kitchen table to work out the cost of the morning and so note this down in her little book in which she kept her weekly budget.

Looking back, things seemed to be cheaper, but this was only a fleeting and very relative concept. For example, in the 1950's: bread cost about eight pence a large loaf; bottled milk was about sixpence a pint; sugar was about five pence a pound bag; butter was about two shillings a pound; potatoes about the same; and tea was about three shillings a pound bag. Most cheap cuts of meats were about a shilling per pound but some special steaks and chops could go up to two shillings but chicken was more expensive.

A letter could be sent around the country for about three pence with two deliveries to the home letter box each day. A telephone call from the tall, red phone box on the corner would cost a penny for a local call. Then again, the average working man only earned about six or seven pounds per week.

Originally our currency in 1950 consisted of two half-pennies, (ha'pnies) made a penny; three pennies were called thrippence or a trey; six pennies were called a zac and twelve pennies made a shilling or a bob. Twenty shillings made a pound (not the weight) or a quid. Going to school, Mum would give me three copper pennies; one each for the tram fare there and back and one penny for a bag of sweets at the Tuck Shop at school. Being very thrifty, my friends and I would walk to school and back and use the entire swag on sweets.

Going into town with Nanna was always an adventure.

The Billy Cart Mechanic

Shopping was not the only reason why we went into town; there were many relatives to visit also. Unfortunately, these were often older relatives; maiden aunts and such. They were nice ladies I guess, but they all seemed to have overdone it with the scented powder and arthritis cream. They also had a desire to kiss and hug small boys and I was the obvious target during these visits. Ugh!

One place to visit was entirely agreeable and very pleasant to me. This was the small cottage on Polding Street which belonged to Mum's cousin, who being an adult was called Uncle Bob. Uncle Bob also worked for the Country Roads Department as a mechanic in their depot just down the street. His job was to repair and maintain all of the interesting heavy machinery which he called plant. His wife was Aunt Ngairie which was pronounced Nerry but had a funny spelling; well at least to my experience of the usual girls' names. Mum said that she was from 'across the ditch' and at the time I found that difficult to understand. What ditch? It took me a while and many repeated questions at school to find that this term referred to the Tasman Sea and that

Aunt Ngairie was from New Zealand. She was a big, happy person and it was rare not to see her broad face lit up by a huge smile.

Uncle Bob and Aunt Ngairie had three children: Amelia who was about my age; Hannah who was a few years older and Harry who had reached big boy status at fourteen. All seemed to have inherited their mother's strong, outgoing nature and were always ready to have a go at most things. Harry was just plain reckless. He boasted that he was going on to finish school next year and get an apprenticeship to be a mechanic like his father. He was already into constructing and pulling things apart and currently his mind revolved around building the ultimate billy cart.

Now, one must remember that in the 1950's and for many years before that, billy carts were one of the prime sources of entertainment for children. It was an institution for every neighbourhood in the city and all over the country for groups of junior mechanics to construct these unwieldy vehicles.

The original billycart came from somewhere well back in history when small carts were made to be pulled by billy goats. Of course, by now the use of goats as a source of propulsion had also disappeared into the diffuse fog of history, except perhaps in the deep north of Queensland where many of the older traditions still sometimes prevailed.

Originally, it was a simple platform with four wheels and a moveable front steering board based on a length of good four-by-two timber with a fixed rear axle on a smaller wooden plank at right-angles across the main beam. The front axle was also on a similar smaller plank but this was made to swivel by a nut and bolt which went through it and through the main beam. Usually, a low wooden box or just a simple wooden plank as a seat was nailed onto the main beam over the rear plank.

It was the choice of wheels which determined the level of expertise of the billy cart maker. Often, the city kid would simply use a set of wheels purchased from the local hardware store at great expense from their meagre pocket money. These were the type of wheels which commonly showed up on laundry trolleys and the like but often they were not suitable for heavy loads as back wheels and were really only suitable for the steering wheels at the front.

Out in the country, the billy cart was more of a heavy-duty art form because most country kids had access to old machinery and other interesting bits of metal work found in the old farm shed or on the town dump. Country kids became the masters of billy cart construction and usually graduated to being deft farm hands or bush mechanics who could rebuild a car engine miles from anywhere with just a screwdriver and a piece of bailing wire.

In the country, the most common and free source of construction material was to be found at the town dump. Saturday morning was the main social event at the dump as most people came there to dump their discarded rubbish but usually went home with more than they had brought. All sorts of valuable items were taken to the dump and many taken back home by others. It was a type of social interaction with recycling. Old bricks, window frames, lengths of timber, crockery, old car and tractor parts and many things which were not needed by one household or business. These were often taken up by others who found such items useful in their own constructions at home. There were no professional scroungers at these dumps nor were there any pretensions of recycling and people were free to take away whatever they found. The town simpleton, Morrie, for example collected bottles and was a master at burrowing into the older sections of the dump to retrieve ancient glassware. These were often worth a small fortune from the gullible types who came down from the city to buy such items, especially from someone who appeared to be simple of mind. Simpleton? Not likely! He knew what he collected and could describe the use, features and a rough estimate of the cost of most bottles. Heaven help any antique dealer from Sydney who tried to put the con on Morrie. The artful bottle collector would simply give the flask buyer an idiotic grin put the bottle away until the price came near to his estimate which was pretty close to the city value less a small percentage to satisfy the purchaser.

Old push-type lawnmower wheels were a premium item to the young billy cart engineers. These were heavy, cast iron spoked wheels about ten inches across and were of a solid construction. Fitted to the ends of old axles, they were ideal for the major load-bearing back wheels. Timber, especially small wooden boxes and lengths of hardwood used in housing construction – the proverbial four-by-two could also be found at the dump.

The other valuable item necessary for billy cart construction were ball bearings. These were small, round concentric circles of steel or races separated by enclosed steel balls and generally were used to reduce friction in machinery with rotating shafts. Usually these could be found at the local garage or farm machinery mechanics where they were regularly being replaced. Old ball-races, as they were also called, made ideal front wheels if they were large enough – say about four or five inches across.

With a set of lawnmower wheels, ball races, a length of four-by-two, some sturdy cross planks, a good nut and bolt and a length of rope to act as reins on the from wheels, all of the materials for a billy cart were ready for the construction. It only needed the innovative genius of the young mind to put them together into a creative mechanical art form.

Reckless Harry, the eldest of Uncle Bob and Aunt Ngairie's three children, was just such a billy cart mechanic. Being one of the older cousins, he roamed freely around the countryside, including the dump, and was also well known at all of the garages and farm machinery outlets in the town. He was a popular young scrounger and as his dad worked for the Country Roads Department (CRD), there were often free interchanges of services, shall we say!

One day, when Nanna and Mum visited Aunt Ngairie for morning tea, I found Reckless busy at work in the backyard shed on his latest creations.

"What a beauty!" he said, standing back from the rather large contraption sitting on the shed's concrete floor. His younger sisters Amelia and Hannah had other thoughts and stood back at some distance smirking to themselves.

"It'll never work, if you ask me," said Hannah the eldest.

"No one did!" snapped Reckless, putting the finishing touches to the heavy bolt on the axle beam.

I looked over Amelia's shoulders and saw the item which was being discussed. It was, of course, a billy cart, but not like any that I had ever seen. This one was over six feet long with two solid-looking mower wheels on the back and two large ball-races on the front. Nothing unusual about that! It was the rest of the cart which was impressive. Reckless had managed to 'borrow' two machinery crates from his father's store of large wooden boxes which he often brought home from his works at the CRD yard just down the road. They were sturdy timber crates used for transporting tractor parts and were about five feet long and about three feet wide – a good size for a coffin if one wasn't so tall. Their top lids had been removed and one had been lifted up and nailed upside down onto the open top of the other, forming an enclosed cabin. Reckless had cut out one end of the lower box to form a small doorway which faced to the rear. This cabin was then nailed to the undercarriage of the billy cart. With some imagination – and Reckless had plenty of that – one could see some resemblance to an old western stage coach and this is what he called it. We all thought that reckless had seen too many John Wayne movies at the town cinema for his own good.

Now completed and with small, padded seat perched up on top of the cabin at its front and a long set of reins leading up to a bent nail near the seat, the heavy stagecoach was hauled out of the yard and onto the street.

Luckily, Polding Street had only recently been re-tarred, thanks to Uncle Bob and the CRD, and so the ball-races would work just fine on the smooth surface. Whilst they gave an almost frictionless ride on tarred and concrete roads, they were next to useless on dirt and grass. The street also had a gentle slope going down about a hundred yards to Comur Street, the main street which ran through the town.

"Go in! Get in!" Reckless said to us kids who were standing gawking at his contraption on the side of the road. The girls were reluctant to do so. They were always cautious of their brother's mechanical inventions.

"Come on Tom!" he said to me. "You'll be up for it, won't you?"

"Alright." I said, willing to get involved with my new-found cousins and so I climbed through the small hole in the rear of the cabin. The two girls followed and the three of us jostled for some degree of comfort in the small space made by the two attached crates.

There was a wobbling as Reckless climbed up onto the roof of the cabin and took up the reins which went down to the outer ends of the front axle beam.

"Off we go!" he yelled in excitement and flicked the reins as if there were imaginary horses attached to our grand stagecoach.

"Off we go!" he shouted again and jiggled his body forward to get the contraption moving. It remained motionless.

"Aw, get out and give us a shove, Sis!" he yelled from above.

Hannah climbed out of the small rear opening and put her hands up onto the upper rear part of the cabin and gave an almighty shove.

Finally, the massive bulk of the stagecoach began to move. Hannah fell forward onto the bitumen of the road as it did so. Slowly but surely the heavy contraption gathered momentum.

Looking out from the rear door/window, the only view of the outside world, we saw a frustrated Hanna sitting on the road and rapidly receding from our view as our vehicle began to pick up a considerable speed, the loud clatter of the heavy iron mower wheels now beginning to fill our ears. Faster and faster, we went. Hannah was now a long way back, standing now and dusting herself off.

"Bail out! Bail out!" came a sudden panicked voice from above.

Alarmed at the speed at which the heavy billy cart had now achieved, Amelia and I thought that that was good advice and so in a mad scramble of legs and arms, we climbed out of the rear opening; Amelia first as she was much bigger than I. We both in turn fell heavily on the road, my bare knees coming off second best with the hard bitumen surface. We both sat there, on the hard surface of Polding Street and watched in awe as Reckless and his stagecoach trundled off towards the open and dangerous crossing with Comur Street beyond.

Reckless was generally considered a genius when it came to building innovative contraptions but in building his stagecoach, he had followed traditional thought and had forgotten one item which his large-scale innovation now lacked: brakes. Usually, the typical billy cart did not require brakes, as the proximity of the rider meant that one could simply apply the sole of one's foot to both of the front wheels. Naturally, shoes had to be worn for such a special occasion. With the tall size of Reckless' stagecoach however, his feet were much too far away from the front wheels to apply as a brake and so he continued on at ever increasing speed across the main street.

A large road-train carrying two carriages of shuffling and mooing cattle roared past just a few feet after the stagecoach had crossed its path; a small car going in the opposite direction also swerved to avoid the careering contraption. The speeding stagecoach, with Reckless tightly holding the reins like grim death trying to keep it on a straight path, rattled across the main road and into the opposite street. Luckily it too sloped down to the main street and so the stagecoach began to slow down. Reckless then had the common sense to pull over onto the grass where the ball races dug into the turf. The whole apparatus came to a sudden stop and tipped over on its side, throwing its white-faced occupant onto the grass.

The two girls and I carefully ran across the road and came up to our unfortunate billy cart mechanic sitting on the ground looking at the wreck of his invention; the two crates having broken apart and now lay like discarded coffins on the side of the road.

Reckless slowly looked up at us with a dazed, vacant look upon his face.

"Well! That's the last of my billy carts I guess," he said with just a small degree of sadness on his ashen face. Then he suddenly brightened up and said with some new enthusiasm looking at one of the open crates resting against a tree:

"Well now! There's an idea! Perhaps I could branch out and build a tree house!"

The girls looked at me with some degree of horror and I wasn't sure whether falling out of a treehouse or being flattened on the main street by a road train was much of a choice.

The Bush Cricket Match

If there is one thing that could both unite a country or divide its opinion, then that is the religion of sport. In the country, the current sporting event was the next thing discussed after the weather and the saleyard values. Even in times of extreme drought, the hard times would be forgotten - well, for a while anyway – when the subject of sport came up. In times of flood or fire, those other two conditions of normal country life, sport was still important. A man would rather have his prize cricket bat or football jersey saved from a fire or flood than most other things except the family and the dog.

Now, with the summer months in full swing and the grass now as brown as can be, the annual Town versus Country picnic cricket match was on everyone's mind. There were plenty of cricket clubs and pitches in Yass, but Nanna agreed with almost everyone that this annual match was the highlight of the season. It was even suggested that men would leave the bar at the Commercial with a Test Match between England and Australia being broadcasted over the radio just to attend this local match, but Mum thought that this was an exaggeration as such a thing wouldn't happen in the Junction Pub back home.

Everyone in the district spent an enormous amount of time getting ready for this grand event: the men would drag out their cricket whites from some dusty wardrobe then get in some practice, especially those who were good cricketers and belonged to a local amateur team. Now this was a distinct advantage for those of the Town side as most usually belonged to one of the town's many cricket teams. Even Boof belonged to the CRD Cricket Association; a rather pretentious name for the men who worked occasionally for this august body and where Uncle Johnny his father, was its Captain.

The other advantage that the Town team had was that it was able to recruit, on short notice, any of the new and unsuspecting schoolteachers, who had the good luck to be posted to the town from the city. These young men or itinerant intellectuals, as some of the established townsfolk called them, usually had some cricket expertise so that they could assist in the weekly school sports afternoons and physical education training of their pupils. For the most part, these young men were keen to get into some of the social life of the town whilst they did their Country Service before returning to the city. Some stayed on, however, finding country school teaching much more pleasant than being stuck in some inner-city school battle zone. Their female colleagues, often found other interests in the local district, especially in the fresh-faced young sons of wealthy property-owners who were considered a good catch.

The woman folk, both town and country would start baking well before the event and many of them, including Nanna, belonged to that cornucopia of country plenty, the Country Women's' Association (CWA). Batches of biscuits, pumpkin scones, lamingtons[4], butterfly cupcakes and all manner of sandwiches would be made in various church halls and homes throughout the town and in the kitchens of many of the surrounding homesteads. Nanna would have several of her friends over and soon there would be several ladies, including Mum, up to their elbows in large bowls of floury mixture and

---

[4] Small cubes of a square of sponge cake dipped in runny chocolate icing and desiccated coconut popular in Australia and New Zealand. They are believed to be named after either Lord Lamington, who served as Governor of Queensland from 1896 to 1901

producing blocks of lovely-smelling fruit cake and other such delicacies from the wide oven of the fuel stove.

Also, busy well before the event, were Uncle Johnny and his son Boof who would take the CRD tractor-grasscutter and disappear for the day out along the Good Hope Road. Well out of town was a well-known spot near the Murrumbidgee River where the match would be played. This was a favourite picnic spot for the Townies and considered neutral ground for those of the Country Set. Here there was a wide flat patch of ground that had long ago been cleared of trees and scrub and had received tender care by Uncle Johnny and his predecessors ever since the first Town-versus-Country match back in 1880. All that was required now was a quick mow over and some scraping by pick, shovel and hand roller to make up the hallowed cricket pitch of twenty-two yards of hard dust.

Early on the sacred day of the match, Nanna and Mum were again in the kitchen putting all of the essential items of food into large wicker hampers along with napkins, knives, forks, spoons, enamelled mugs and plates. Several metal thermos flasks were brought out from their usual position well back in the cupboard over the sink and placed near the hampers. These would be filled with boiling water from the urn on the stove just before leaving and would be used later to make the copious mugs of tea which would be shared around, mostly to the ladies as the men had other supplies.

Uncle Johnny, having returned from his duties as groundsman had another sacred task to fulfil. This was to haul up the several hessian bags from the well and transfer as many cold bottles of amber fluid as he could pack into the two large tool chests from the CRD. These had been cleaned and packed with ice sprinkled with handfuls of salt added to drop the temperature even further. This was important to keep their precious contents cold all day, but usually when the sun rose higher in the sky out at the field, the number of bottles soon declined rapidly at the hands of thirsty players and supporters. There was also a smaller metal chest filled with ice and bottles of lemonade and creaming soda for us kids as well as several bottles of milk for the tea.

Soon after a big country breakfast, Uncle Bob and Aunt Ngairie and their three children arrived in

Uncle Bob's A-model Ford. This was a small tray top truck consisting of the cabin and a flat, wooden tray at the back. On it Uncle Bob would carry all manner of items such as crates, now emptied of spare parts from the CRD depot, bails of hay for local grazier friends and firewood for any town families who needed it. To me this was a lovely machine as it predated most vehicles which occasionally came down our street back home. Indeed, this small truck probably was one of the oldest vehicles in the town, but it had been lovingly kept in showroom condition by Uncle Bob and his son Reckless.

Uncles Johnny and Bob and Cousin Boof began loading the hampers, metal chests and other useful items such as rugs and jerry cans full of water onto the back of the truck, making sure that there would be a comfortable space in the middle for the womenfolk and us kids to sit during the short journey out to the venue. The three men went into the house and soon re-emerged dressed in their cricket whites ready for action in the Town team.

The drive out to the field was exciting; along the short stretch of bitumen of the town and then the winding, tree-lined dusty dirt roads leading to the picnic spot. I did not get much of an opportunity to ride on the back of trucks back home; most of our transport consisted of the tram and rare taxi ride to one of Mum's brothers who lived in other suburbs in the city. Few people in our street owned a car and so standing up behind the old A-model's cabin hanging on to its back with my cousins with the wind blowing through my hair was quite a thrill.

Our joy was short-lived as Uncle Bob parked the A-model into the far corner of the temporary carpark which Uncle Johnny and Boof had cleared several days before and marked out with small witches' hats, as they called the orange-striped traffic cones, courtesy of the CRD. The men carried the heavy hampers and chests across the pitch over to a spot under the trees just beyond the cleared playing field. Rugs were spread out onto the grass and the ladies settled down to sort out the picnic and to pour out the first of many cups of tea for the day. Soon other parties appeared through the trees and found appropriately-shaded places to spread their blankets or set up their camp chairs. Some came across the field and joined Nanna's party under the trees which lined the river bank behind where we sat. Nanna said that this was the best place to be as it was cooler near the river and on the Leg Side where few big hits are sent so that the peace of their picnic would not be disturbed.

Now, the last few years had not been good for the members of the Country Team. Firstly, there had been the usual drought of several years, followed by the its plague of locusts which ate what was left of the crops and grass and then the bushfires which wiped out the locusts; not to mention some stock, fences, sheds and a few homesteads. Whilst most of the established landowners simply shrugged their shoulders and got on with re-building, some of the younger newcomers and a few valuable farm hands had walked off to seek better pastures elsewhere. These events unfortunately had caused a most monumental disaster; the Country Cricket Team now lacked some of its younger and more able players. Yet another defeat for the Country side at the hands of the flash and experienced Townies loomed large. Even Uncle Errol, who was not noted for his physical activity and interest in sport, except when in the Commercial during race days, had been drafted to join the Country team as the Last Man Jack who would be the last to be called to bat. Of course, no one objected to the fact that he was also running a 'book' on the match and had convinced a large number of gullible punters to bet on a win for the Country team. These unfortunates were either new to the district or were convinced that the Country team must win this time after so many past defeats – the classical gamblers fallacy.

With everyone settled amongst the trees around the oval, as the bare patch of country bush was called with some pretension to hallowed English cricket, the match officially began when the umpire Mr. Ledger waddled pompously out onto the field in his white coat and broad-brimmed hat. He was one of the town's bankers but was not considered much of a friend to any side, being a most austere and humourless man who rarely showed any emotions and so was considered a neutral to both teams.

He had also, once in a rare moment of social interaction, admitted to being on his school cricket team when he was a student at Saint Drogo's College in Sydney. With these qualifications and because no one else wanted the job, he had been made the umpire when he was first transferred to the town several years ago and had kept this position ever since.

Uncle Johnny from the CRD and Big Bill McDonald of Blackwater Station followed him out as the Captains of the two teams to take the toss – the traditional tossing up of a coin to see which team went to bat first up. Uncle Johnny won the toss so he walked back to the Town team to kit up ready to return as the first batsman. Uncle Bill McDonald simply stood on the field and waved his arm for the Country team to come onto the field.

And so, the match started with much enthusiasm from the assembled groups of picnicking supporters under the trees. After a few hours the enthusiasm had died down to stoic observation and Nanna made some comment, whilst pouring yet another cup of tea for Mum, something about watching cricket matches was akin to sitting and watching the grass growing in the dry season.

After a short adjournment for morning tea, which naturally included a significant consumption of lamingtons, butterfly cakes, pumpkin scones, sandwiches and cold bottles of amber fluid, the cricketers returned to their positions on the field. The Town team was already in another commanding position with only five batsmen out for one hundred and five runs and Uncle Errol was already mentally counting the takings from his betting activities as he strode out to his fielding position at the very far end of the oval.

A new bowler came out onto the pitch for the Country team. He was a very young man who was unknown to most of the spectators and so there was some renewed interest in the game. He was young Hamish McDonald, a nephew of Big Bill and had recently returned home for the Christmas holidays from W.C. Grace College in Sydney, a superior Greater Public School (GPS) where he had been a senior boarder. He had also been the gun all-rounder for the college's First XI cricket team who had won the GPS competition that very year.

When the first wicket fell for a duck[5], the Townie supporters put down their tea or beer and sat up and paid attention to what now was going on at the pitch. After a few stumbling runs another wicket fell and the Townies knew that they were in trouble. Finally, the last wicket fell for only an extra twenty-two runs and the teams retired for an early lunch;

---

[5] Slang expression in cricket meaning that the batsman was out for zero runs.

the Country team slapping their young bowler on the back with grins of triumph on their faces and the Townie batsmen walking off with heads hung low and dragging their bats behind them.

The happy picnic atmosphere had now changed with great apprehension appearing within the Town set and some obvious joy in the supporters of the invigorated Country team; a lot more amber fluid appeared for different reasons in both camps. Uncle Errol now sat morosely under a small tree estimating his potential losses should his team do the unthinkable and win – especially since he had himself backed the Town team at odds of ten-to-one on with another bookie.

The opening Country batsmen put on their pads, picked up their bats and strode confidently onto the pitch; the Town team wandered out to their assigned fielding positions with Boof coming over to near where Nanna, Mum and I were sitting in the trees not far from the river. He muttered something about the Country team's new ring-in and accepted another lamington before retreating a few paces back to assume his casual position in the deep field.

After taking a few wickets for a modest number of runs by the opposition, the Townies called out their top bowler to deal with young Hamish McDonald who had now taken his position as sixth bat.

"Just you watch Nobby bowl this kid out," said Boof from his position not far from us. Nobby, or Mr. Walsh as his class called him to his face, was well known for his expertise at the local High School where he coached the Under Fifteen team who were the current Monaro District Champions. He was also noted for his skill the cane in class as well as with the bat on the pitch so his many former pupils watching today thought that his aggressiveness would soon take care of young Hamish.

"Whack!" the first ball, a fast bowl to the off stump had been dealt a tremendous blow from young Hamish's bat and the ball now soared well over the head of the fieldsman at cover and into the trees beyond. The umpire, Mr. Ledger kept his statue-like expression and raised both arms above his head to signal a boundary six runs. Things were not looking good for the Townies but a new spark of optimism came to the supporters of the Country team.

The match throughout that afternoon became one of intense interest to the supporters of both teams. The County side now had some hope that for once their team might win and bring some forgotten joy to the struggling families on the land. The Townies were confronted with the simple realisation and horror that they might even lose. Eventually, with the runs piling up for the Country team, young Hamish was caught out by a lucky catch from Uncle Bob who was at the Long Off position. Young Hamish walked off the pitch waving his bat triumphantly and grinning, having scored a creditable eighty-five runs.

The next batsmen for the Country team now had a confidence which they had never experienced before and so strode out to the wicket with a new hope. Another thirty-eight runs were put onto the board until the ninth batsman, Mixo Anderson, got out for a duck. This left only Uncle Errol to bat and the hope by the Country team that they might scrape through and achieve a long sought-after victory faded. Errol McDonald was not considered to be much of a sportsman and was generally regarded as being totally useless at most other things as well. Supporters on the Country side cursed and turned to more amber fluid or yet another cup of tea to drown their disbelief and sorrows. The Townie supporters suddenly perked up as did Uncle Errol's punters who now calculated what their bets at high odds would earn.

These feelings of dread or hope from the respective sides only increased as Uncle Errol came onto to the pitch and faced the demon bowler Nobby Walsh. There were gasps of disbelief as Uncle Errol faced the bowler as a left-handed batsman -a south paw. Uncle Errol seemed to be sinister in more ways than one.

Shock and horror spread throughout the Country team. Nanna turned to Mum and casually remarked:

"He's only left-handed when you give him a bat or a club. Usually, he is right-handed in all other things. His mother thinks that the schoolteachers made him be like the other children and taught him to write in the proper way when he was young."

Mum simply nodded her head as this seemed to be just the way of things and that being left-handed was a sad handicap for a young boy.

On the field, the appearance of a left-hander would often mean some rearrangement of the fieldsmen, especially if the batsman was any good and therefore more open places of the field on the leg side needed to be covered. But Uncle Johnny simply didn't bother and kept his fieldsmen where they were. He simply knew that Uncle Errol had as about much chance of hitting the ball in that direction as his son Boof, who was innocently standing on the deep leg side not far from us, had of catching it.

Never-the-less, there was now significant tension in the air with only one ball in the last over left, and four runs for a draw. There were even a few religious types on the Country side who hoped and prayed for a miracle from Uncle Errol.

Nobby took a long run up after looking around with the same expression of satisfaction on his face as when he delivered six-of-the best whilst caning his most errant pupils.

A bumper! The ball came speeding out of his hands and hit the dirt pitch in a cloud of flying dust at some distance before Uncle Errol. For his part, he saw it coming and with some fear in his heart he closed his eyes and took a mighty swing at the air with his bat. Now, whether it was simply luck, good fortune or the answer to the prayers of the religious group of the Country set, the ball and bat made contact.

Whack!

The ball went high into the air and headed to where Boof was casually standing gazing at nothing in particular. He woke up and saw the small, red shape rapidly coming for him.

Panic!

He tried to follow the ball and so he ran along the tree line at the edge of the field hoping to make a catch and save the game. The ball flashed over his out-stretched arms and into the trees.

Whack!

It hit a large hornet's nest just above where Boof finally came to a halt.

Confusion!

Hornets and the shattered remains of their nest flew everywhere, especially around the head of the unbelieving Boof.

Confusion!

Everyone in their little picnics panicked!

Boof took fright and wisely headed off at a great speed no one would give him credit for, through the trees to the river beyond and safety from the stinging hornets.

Nanna, Mum, Cousin Gemina who had come over to heckle her fielding cousin and I all ducked under the picnic blanket sending lamingtons, butterfly cakes, pumpkin scones, sandwiches and crockery flying. The rest of the picnickers on our side also jumped up with alarm as did many of the others on the other side of the oval. The cricketers generally ran about wondering if they should stay on the field or go to their families who were now running about on the edge of the field.

Uncle Errol had recovered from his accidental but monumental hit and anticipating the worst, now thought that it was a convenient time during such mass panic to 'do a runner'. He dropped his offending bat, turned and lumbered off the field still wearing his batsman's pads towards his little coupe in the car park hoping to escape his many creditors.

In the middle of this pandemonium, umpire Ledger was standing firm behind the batsman's wicket with his usual statue-like expression and raised both

arms above his head to signal a boundary six runs.
The country team had finally won.

Christmas at Auchenblae

It was almost Christmas and there were reminders all over the town. There were decorations in the shop windows and talk of the coming season of goodwill. I had mixed feelings of both apprehension and joy about Christmas: my father had died just before last Christmas and so that had been a time of sadness and mourning.

Celebrating Christmas was not on my mind until Uncle Johnny came through the front door one morning dragging a huge pine tree by its freshly cut stem.

"Here ya are!" he said to me with a cheerful smile. "The first of the Christmas trees."

I looked at the large, green tree lying on the polished dark wood floor of the front parlour and then out through the door where a grinning Boof stood standing next to the CRA truck which now had a large green mass of similar trees tied to its flat bed.

"Well, back to work!" he continued as he went back out to the truck.

Nanna explained that Uncle Johnny and Boof always went out about this time along the Murrumbateman road to cut Christmas trees. There was a large pine plantation on this road which ran south from Yass to the nation's capital in Canberra, and aerial seeding meant that many trees grew along the side of the road outside of the plantation's fence line.

Uncle Johnny and Boof, when he joined the CRD, would go out every year and cut down a truckload of the best sized pine trees and bring them into town. After delivering them free of charge to the most needy of families around the district, and this included Aunt Hannah and all of the relatives, he and Boof would then set up a stand on the side of Comur Street near the small park in the town and sell the remainder to passers-by.

"A nice little earner!" Boof had exclaimed to me later that day. Christmas preparation had begun in earnest.

Nanna and Mum had then dragged the tree over to one side near the fireplace of the front parlour. With a little effort, we lifted it up and planted it into an old, empty kerosene drum which had had its top completely cut off and its interior washed out. This we had filled with compacted earth which I had brought in as several bucketfuls from the paddock. Nanna then draped some coloured Christmas wrapping paper from last year around the outside of the drum and the tree was now set for decoration.

We always had a tree at home at Christmas, except for last year, but it had always been a much smaller version of the giant which now almost reached the ceiling in Nanna's from parlour. In the Junction, our tree was usually purchased from the local fruit and vegetable shop and carried home attached to Mum's shopping cart. Here, we would use the old decorations from previous years which Mum kept in a box on the floor of the linen cupboard. She had originally bought them from Hanrahan's Toy Shop up the hill on Maroubra Road, but lately they seemed to have faded somewhat in their sparkle and appeal.

Here at Auchenblae, Nanna also had a cardboard box filled with some of the more exciting items of Christmas decoration: bundles of brightly-coloured, sparkling tinsel; delicate red glass balls; striped candy canes; coloured ribbons; and of course, a small, crystal angel to be mounted on the very top of the tree. Other decorations such as paper streamers were hung all around the front parlour and a large, ivy wreath decorated with fake white, shiny snow, was placed on the outside of the front door. Nanna also made up some fake snow from baking powder and water and smeared it around the outside edges of the two windows in the front of the house and on the small, coloured panes of the front door. I had never seen real snow, except in photographs and at the movies, so I always wondered what it would be like.

Uncle Stanley, who rarely left his bed, was in charge of making the brightly-colour Christmas stars which would be hung onto the ends of the branches. I helped him cut these shapes out of silver and gold cardboard which Nanna had bought at the newspaper shop earlier that week. He had a tray covered with newspaper sitting on his lap and would dab a little glue on each star and I would then sprinkle on some multi-coloured glitter to complete the decoration. This operation generally worked well, although the smell and smoke from Uncle Stanley's old pipe seemed to distract from the task in hand. He also thought it appropriate to tell me of his time in the Great War; not the one which had finished only a few years back, but the First World

War for which he and his brothers had volunteered all of those years ago. He and his brother Bill came back but his brother Jack was still buried somewhere in France. The Great War had started only thirteen years after our country had been founded and for a young country of only five million people, over sixty thousand had not returned, this was a huge loss.

The other thing which I found distressing during this time of preparation was the killing of the chickens. One day, not long after the delivery of the Christmas trees and a few days before Christmas, Uncle Johnny returned with two live chickens in his grasp. They were tied by the legs and weakly flapping their wings in guttural protest. He took them out to the wood pile where the chopping block and axe were sitting next to the pile of wood for the stove. Luckily, I had already collected the bucket of wood chips and pile of kindling for fuel early that morning. There were a series of loud squawks and then silence.

Uncle Johnny then soaked the bodies in hot water in the large washing tub on the back veranda and after what seemed to be a very long time, began to pluck out all of the feathers. I can still remember the musty, gamey smell of the wet feathers, even today and chicken rarely features in my diet. Back home, Mum would occasionally buy a chicken from our local butcher, but they came already processed, filled with stuffing, bagged and were, at that time, considered an expensive item to be had only on special occasions.

Having cleaned and gutted the two chickens, Uncle Johnny handed them to nanna for stuffing. Naturally, she did not slaughter her own brood of egg-layers who always seemed to be absent about this time, hiding somewhere in the long grass of the overgrown paddock. Now, Nanna would make up the stuffing from crumbs from an old loaf of stale bread which had been kept out for such occasion as well as chopped onion, celery, herbs, egg and some of the giblets kept when the chickens were cleaned. The chickens were then roasted in the big oven of the fuel stove and put aside in the Coolgardie safe to be eaten cold on the day.

Next came the ritual of making the Christmas puddings. Mum and Nanna got busy in the hot kitchen with large mixing bowls and all of the necessary ingredients: flour; raisons and sultanas; glace cherries; eggs; butter; cinnamon; and of course, a large dose of sweet-smelling rum which Nanna generously poured into the bowls from a small bottle which she kept hidden away from Boof in the cupboard. Once the doughy masses were thoroughly mixed, they were stuffed full of three-penny pieces which Nanna also kept in a jar in the same cupboard for each Christmas. Some of these small coins had once been silver but now their lustre had diminished to almost a black colour. Those that were not scavenged by the children from previous years were recovered, washed and stored for next time. I noticed that most of the threepences were still bright and shiny meaning that they had been only recently added to the collection. The scavenging had been particularly thorough the previous years and I meant to get my share this time. I did not particularly like Christmas pudding then, but the thought of obtaining some hard currency appealed to me and so I would have to suffer by eating some of the pudding. The only other delight for me with Christmas pudding was when it was ready to be served up. Nanna would pour brandy over the top of the pudding and light it with a match. The light blue flame would dance around on the top of the puddings adding some extra cheer to the gathering.

Christmas in Australia, both town and country, when the temperature in mid-summer was often well over one hundred degrees Fahrenheit, still persisted in following English tradition and was had as a baked dinner at lunch with the extended family. All of the trappings, including the decorated tree, snow-covered windows and the hot baked vegetables with pork, ham and cold chicken was often also supplemented by large amounts of cooked prawns as the representative seafood. This was particularly the fare back home in the city where prawns were ready obtainable though expensive. In the country, they were not so easily obtained, but a few nights of yabby hunting often produced an acceptable substitute. These freshwater crayfish were cooked up in tall rectangular tins previously used to store honey and were considered quite a delicacy amongst my relatives. However, yabbies were things to be caught rather than eaten as far as I was concerned.

For such a grand cooking event, Nanna, Mum and I would have to make a special trip into town to purchase all that would be necessary for cooking. I could not understand why Mum asked me to go with Nanna off to the various stores whilst she went to get some special items. Many years later I finally realised that this was the only time that my poor mother had to slip away and buy presents for me and the rest of the family. We would return home with the old shopping trolley, which Nanna dragged behind her along the dusty track along the Good Hope Road, full of all sorts of packages, bottles and bags. Mum also carried a large string bag full of suspicious rectangular boxes wrapped tightly in brown paper.

The night before Christmas, Nanna and Mum finished off the cooking and then Nanna hung up four large socks along the wooden mantel piece over the large, open fireplace of the front parlour. These were really old, grey woollen socks taken from Uncle Stanley's drawer many years ago and washed thoroughly until they were almost threadbare. Back home, Mum often hung up some old pillow cases instead. Christmas stockings were an important part of my Christmas and I hoped that I had been considered sufficiently good that year so that Santa Claus would fill them with presents and not potatoes or an old apple in retribution.

It was a wondrous time for me and I was excited on Christmas Eve that this day had finally come. The true meaning of Christmas was not a big feature of our family; a quick visit to the local church would probably come tomorrow but that was a long time away. Nanna gave me a small plate of biscuits and a glass of her precious sherry to put under the stockings on the hearth of the fireplace. This was for Santa to collect when he came down the chimney later that night, being a very curious child, I wondered how such a grand personage, as seen on all of the Christmas wrapping, would survive the night with thousands of biscuits and glasses of sherry in the offering. I had seen Mum's younger brother, Uncle Eustace drunk on sherry on several festive occasions, so I was worried how Santa would also fare.

Just before bed, and being too excited to sleep, I went out onto the front veranda and looked up into the sky hoping to see the glimmer of a sleigh and its team of reindeer. Nothing but thousands of bright, flashing stars of all colours. Not the dull sky of the city back home. The thought occurred to me that Santa would also have problems landing on our tin roof. The corrugated iron heated up to a very high temperature during the day and probably would not be cool enough for the feet of his reindeer who were used to pulling the sleigh around the snow-covered fields which also figured prominently on all of the wrapping paper. Well, he was magic I hoped, and so could do things which others could not do, including fitting his large red bulk down our old chimney in the front parlour. Then off to bed full of many thoughts of a jolly, red-suited figure landing on a hot tin roof and squeezing his great bulk down a narrow chimney and having to drink yet another glass of sherry, Sleep came with great difficulty that night forced only by the promise of presents the next morning.

Dawn, and its cool, grey light came creeping into our bedroom at the back of the house. The neighbour's rooster was yet to alert everyone to the rising of the sun. I flung the sheet off and jumped out of bed and quietly crept into the front parlour. In our family, there was no tradition of waiting until everyone had returned from church nor even after everyone had arisen; it was every boy for himself on Christmas morning!

Out to the front parlour and to the end stocking which Mum and put up just for me.

Empty!

A sudden feeling of dejection filled my heart until I saw the red cardboard arrow pinned to the outside of the stocking. It pointed down to a large rectangular box wrapped in bright Christmas paper of Santa heads, sleighs, snow and Christmas canes. No mercy here! The lovely paper, so carefully wrapped, was torn apart to reveal a large box of Meccano, that junior engineering system of nuts, bolts and flat metal shapes that could be put together to construct all sorts of interesting things. I noticed very briefly that Santa had accepted his biscuits and sherry and that the other socks were filled with bulky shapes.

It was the custom then, especially for people with limited funds, to give only one present to each member of the family. The mass distribution of useless items of commercialised Christmas had yet to dawn on the childhood of young Australians. We were happy to receive just the one present from our parents. Then again, there were others in our extended family who would soon arrive for Christmas lunch and I was sure that they would not arrive empty handed. Afterall, we had put out presents under the Christmas tree for each of my many uncles, aunts and cousins.

As soon as we had returned from the simple church service at the old wooden church on the edge of town, Mum and Nanna got busy cooking and generally making the place ready for their guests. The large table in the front parlour was now moved out into the centre of the room and chairs were brought in from all over the house. Another long table further down the room was made by placing a long, wide piece of timber onto two wooden sawhorses and covered with a white tablecloth. This would be for us kids and it was soon decorated with bowls of lollies, potato crisps and later small bottles of unopened icy cold soft drink from the well. Plates, cups and cutlery were placed all around both tables and the smell of the baked vegetables soon permeated the whole house.

The first guests to arrive were the family from Blackwater Station; Uncle Big Bill McDonald, his wife Aunt Mavis, his daughter Cousin Gemina and her brother Blackie who generally thought that Christmas, like Dicken's famous character was a load of humbug. Uncle Errol was there too, having returned from the city where he had been on business. Nanna had quietly said to Mum that this business trip included making some astute investments at the track at Randwick Racecourse and that he could now pay his creditors from the cricket match.

Uncle Bill had brought a large hamper on his truck which he and his brother Uncle Errol now carried into the warm kitchen. In it was a large ham and side of pork. He explained to Nanna that the wild pigs on his property had been most prolific that year and he had trapped a few of the piglets in his trap before they had the chance to develop intestinal worms common to the adults. He was quite proud of his catch. He had made a spiral-shaped trap out of pig-mesh to trap the wild pigs which dug up his fences and sometimes killed his lambs. Two of the piglets he had kept whilst the adults had been shot and burned as an introduced pest. He had killed and dressed the piglets and now they were to be part of our Christmas lunch. The roast pork was reheated in the oven and I really loved the crackling. To me, things were getting even better and there were also some small gifts from the Blackwater family.

Others soon arrived, including Uncle Johnny and Boof, who after a cherry "Merry Christmas" got on to the most important part of the morning; the hauling out of the many bags of bottles which Uncle Johnny and been hoarding down the old well along the little track at the rear of the house. There would be plenty of amber fluid for the adults as well as cold bottles of lemonade and creaming soda for us kids.

Soon we were all settled at the tables in the front parlour. All of my cousins, both real and honourable, both big boys and little and at the main table, Mum, Nanna and all of the uncles and aunts who made up this extended happy country family. Soon there were the sounds of many Christmas crackers exploding around both tables and the laughter of the family as they put on their small paper crowns and read out the rather lame jokes which were written on small slips of paper inside the crackers. Lunch was a very happy affair with large amounts of wondrous food, talking with all of my cousins and watching my mother now happy and laughing with all of her family.

Suddenly back in the present, I was woken out of my daydream about Auchenblae those many years ago by the pleasant gurgling and melodic sounds of the currawong outside of my study window. Here I was back at my desk at the university with still all of those Final Term papers to mark. But now my spirit had been renewed as it had been back then when my mother and I had found a new life in the small cottage on the road to Good Hope.

Other Books by the Author

Fiction

Tom Shipley Series (Humour)

The Innocence of Tom Shipley: Teacher
A 19 year old teacher reports to his first school to find that he is the Acting Head of Department. He meets many interesting characters in his first years of teaching.

Tom Shipley's War Memoirs of a Weekend Warrior 1965 and the first ballot for Australian conscripts for the Vietnam War. With many of his friends drafted and the protest movement now directed against them, Tom Shipley enlists into the local Army Reserve unit and finds a new enemy; the Army itself.

Tall Ships Series (Historical Science Fiction)

The Ice Ship 1840 and an advanced steam-auxiliary whaling ship sets out from New England to go whaling in Antarctic waters. A freak storm of cold weather sends it further south and it becomes embedded in the ice. Panicked, the crew desert and leave their young captain on board. This is a tale about their survival.

Two Hundred Years Before the Mast, An Adventure in Time It is 1996 and a young Nuclear

Physicist accidently discovers how to travel in time. Having an interest in the days of fighting sail, he goes back to the year 1796 where he is unexpectedly press ganged aboard a Royal Navy frigate. How does he survive the peril in which his ship is placed?

San Rafael Series (Historical Adventure - written as Hernan Moreno Ruiz)

Letters from San Rafael It is 1880 and Peruvian intelligence officer, Colonel Moreno and his Sergeant, Garcia, are captured by the Ecuadorians during a border dispute and taken to the supply depot of San Rafael in Ecuador. Treated as guests by the old Comandante, Moreno is able to smuggle letters home. They each tell a separate tale about South America and its people at that time as told to Morano by the people of San Rafael.

Return to San Rafael Ten years on and Moreno and Garcia are called upon by their former captors to return to the now deserted hacienda of San Rafael to discover its secret which will affect the future of both Peru and Ecuador. Along the way they hear many stories of the places through which they travel and meet the mysterious Father Xavier, a Jesuit priest who knows more about their secret mission than they do.

Confessions of Father Xavier Set in the 1870's, this is the story of how a young Peruvian cavalry officer becomes the mysterious Jesuit priest, Father Xavier and the many adventures he has before becoming an agent for both the Church and Government.

Australian Bush Stories (Short Stories)

Cry of the Currawong Australian country life in the 1950's and how a young boy from the city finds many adventures with his new-found cousins, uncles and aunts.

Non-Fiction

Survival Series

A Pocketbook of Hiking and Survival A pocket encyclopedia of survival skills for the outdoors designed to be carried in pocket or pack.

A Pocketbook of Surviving Teaching and Instruction A guide for all teachers and Instructors, sometimes in a humous vein and based on over 40 years of experience in teaching and instruction.

Surviving Global Warming: A Guide for the Future A complete guide to climate change both natural and man made with special reference to resources and energy. Each chapter has a personal how to survive section.

Adventures in Earth Science Series

Adventures in Earth Science (compendium issue)

A complete encyclopedia about the Earth and beyond written with over 40 years of experience and travels on all seven continents. Over 800 pages with 1500 photos and illustrations and more than 30 video links taken by the author in his adventurous travels. This series also comes with a **Teachers' Guide** and **Student Practical Manual.**

This large (A4 sized) textbook has been broken up into a series of eight small-sized books for easier reading by everyone age 12+. The series includes:

Exploration Science Field Geology and Mapping

Riches from the Earth, Minerals, Energy and Mining

A Dangerous Planet Volcanoes and Earthquakes

Changing the Surface Erosion and Landscapes

Rocks- Building the Earth Rocks and their formation

Fossils -Life in the Rocks Studying ancient life and its environment

Through Sea and Sky, Oceanography and Meteorology

Beyond Planet Earth, an Introduction to Astronomy A complete guide to studying the universe.

Adventures in Earth and Environmental Science Series

An extension of the previous series with emphasis on the Earth and its changing environments both in climate and on the surface. It comes as two large (A4) textbooks based on the Australian nation syllabus in Environmental Science. Each volume comes with a Student Practical Manual, there is also a Teachers' Guide.

Adventures in Earth and Environmental Science Book 1

Adventures in Earth and Environmental Science Book 2

About the Author

Peter Scott was born and raised in Sydney by country parents. Trained as a teacher, he spent many years in country schools teaching Science before moving to Queensland where he now lives with his wife, children and grandchildren. He has travelled to many parts of the world and was a Queensland Teacher of the Year in 2008 before retiring after over forty years in the profession. He holds several post-graduate research degrees and was a former Army Reserve Officer.

9 781925 662443